Remember Me

Also by Sarah Diamond

The Beach Road
Cold Town

Remember Me

Sarah Diamond

ORION

First published in Great Britain in 2002 by Orion,
an imprint of the Orion Publishing Group Ltd.

Copyright © Sarah Diamond 2002

The moral right of Sarah Diamond to be identified as the
author of this work has been asserted in accordance
with the Copyright, Designs and Patents Act of 1988.

A CIP catalogue record for this book is
available from the British Library.

ISBN 0 75285 360 0 (hardback) 0 75285 361 9 (trade paperback)

Typeset by Deltatype Ltd, Birkenhead, Merseyside

Set in Minion

Printed in Great Britain by
Clays Ltd, St Ives plc

The Orion Publishing Group Ltd
Orion House
5 Upper Saint Martin's Lane
London, WC2H 9EA

To Kate and Michelle,
who inspired this novel in Leicester Square

Book One

Don't know where to start, or what to say. Don't even know why it matters. I'll have to tear it up as soon as I've finished. Can't have them finding it.

But I had to write it down. Otherwise, it's going to drive me mad. I just found out she's going away for two weeks, next Wednesday. Leaving me with Him.

It's funny, really. Started off today in such a good mood, because nothing had happened yesterday or the day before, or even the day before that, and I thought I'd found a way to hide from him. Lately, I've been sticking to her like a limpet, and even though I don't like her as much as I did, it feels sort of like having a bodyguard. As long as she's there, I'm safe – he won't do anything in front of her.

And then this afternoon, she says she's going away for two weeks.

She sounded so happy, like a little kid. I never knew you could say something that almost gives someone else a heart attack and not have the least idea. Guess what, she said, we're going to – and I just froze up and stared at her. Don't worry, she smiled, I'll send you a postcard, and I swear to God I just wanted to kill her. Because she doesn't understand, and there's no way I can tell her that she was smiling about something that's going to keep me awake every night till they leave.

I know it's not her fault. But that doesn't seem to matter. Before this all started, I thought someone had to do something bad to upset you, but they don't. It's enough for them just to be there, happy when you're terrified, not even seeing you're terrified, not knowing there's any reason to be. Like living in a nightmare with someone who's living in a

3

dream. Lately, when I see her smile, I wish she was dead.

Of course, I don't mean that. I can't. Before all this, we were best friends.

Whatever he did to me last week, it's going to be ten times worse when she's gone. I know that much for a fact. While she's off having a lovely time.

But I don't hate her. Really.

I don't hate her—

1

She woke up abruptly. For a second or two, though she couldn't remember the dream she'd just had, it was still oddly strong in her mind – a taste she couldn't put any immediate name to, an echo that could have been caused by anything at all.

She reached out to touch the sleeping man beside her – turned, rested her chin on one hand as she looked down at him. Saw a roundish, blunt-featured face peaceful in sleep, tousled sandy-blond hair against the pillow. She felt a sudden, intense rise of tenderness, and shook him gently, with a half-recognised urge to banish the misty remnants of the dream.

'Andrew. *Andrew.*'

She watched him slowly surface from sleep, eyes opening – grey-blue eyes, weary, humorous, slightly naive. 'What's the matter?'

'Nothing.' She felt embarrassed at having woken him, even as part of her was reassured. 'I'll have to get up in a minute.'

'Half six already?' He reached out for her, drew her into a sleepy and asexual cuddle which she melted into gratefully. 'How come you always manage to wake up before the alarm?'

'Just a natural talent, I guess.' They lay together in peaceful half-lit silence for long minutes before she spoke again. 'Better start getting ready. I'll be late for work.'

'Surely they'd let you get away with that today? The star of the Fanta pitch?' She laughed. He pulled her closer to him. 'Come on, sweetheart, stay in here a bit longer. No rush.'

'You know I want to. I just can't.' She disengaged her flesh from his with genuine regret. 'I've got that lunch with the boss later, and for all I know, she's going to keep me for *hours* – I'll have to get a lot of work out of the way this morning.'

'You're too responsible for your own good sometimes,' Andrew grinned. 'Puts me to shame.' And she smiled too, getting out of bed, barefooting her way across the stripped-pinewood floor, heading into the bathroom, where she washed and brushed herself ready to face the day. A bright May morning showed through the half-open blinds, and the light was dazzling.

Back in the bedroom, Andrew was still in bed. Rachel went over to the wardrobe to get dressed and dropped the towel she'd wrapped round herself, prompting a slow, appreciative wolf-whistle from behind her. She laughed, turned. 'Hadn't you better get a move on?' she asked, buttoning up her blouse. 'You'll be late for work yourself, one of these days.'

'Never happens. You must know that by now.'

He spoke airily – it was true, she knew, he never seemed to go out of his way to get things done, but it all fell into place for him just the same. She often had a sense that she was older than him, even though she was nearly two years his junior. 'Just born lucky,' she retorted, pulling the curtains wide open to let the sun in.

She was putting on her make-up at the dressing table when she heard him padding into the bathroom, showering, starting to sing. An involuntary smile touched the edges of her lips. 'Do you do encores?' she called, but couldn't tell whether he'd heard her over the running water. She applied a second coat of mascara, and made the bed with a chambermaid's precision.

In the kitchen, she poured herself black coffee, which was all the breakfast she ever had, and noticed the open jar of Nutella on the side, the tell-tale crumbs that told her Andrew had succumbed to an attack of the munchies while she was asleep. A familiar blend of exasperation and deep affection took hold of her as she screwed the lid back on the jar and replaced it in the cupboard, cleaned the crumbs off carefully, wiped down the marble so it gleamed. 'Andrew,' she called, with half-genuine, half-joking irritation. 'Will you *ever* learn?'

He appeared in the door dressing-gowned, vigorously towelling his shower-damp hair. 'Will *you* ever learn to relax?' he complained, taking the cloth from her hand. 'They're *crumbs*. They don't *bite*.'

She couldn't help laughing – he had that effect on her, made her take things less seriously. 'I suppose they *might* run wild, if you let them get out of control,' he continued gravely. 'We'd come back one night to find them rampaging through the flat.'

'I know, I know. It's just a shame to make a mess. It's such a beautiful flat.' Her gaze swept the kitchen with a pleasure that was more than houseproud, before she felt his mocking eyes on her and grinned. 'Anyway, duty calls. I'd better make tracks.'

'See you later,' he said, and pulled her in for a kiss on her way out of the kitchen. She returned it for long seconds, enjoying the Badedas-and-toothpaste taste of him before the ticking clock in her head became impossible to ignore. 'Have a nice day,' she said at last, pulling away.

'You too, sweetheart. And enjoy your lunch with the boss.'

The apartment block they lived in was a private development, and the neat curves of her year-old black MG gleamed in the crowded forecourt. She got in, started the engine and set off.

Her prowess behind the wheel tended to reflect her mood: under stress, she was probably the nerviest and most erratic driver in the capital; this morning, almost as laid-back as Andrew himself. She was cruising out of Camden and humming along to chart music on the radio when the double-decker bus pulled out in front of her without warning, and she'd squealed to a hair's-breadth halt before she was a hundred per cent certain she wasn't dead.

2

Sophie was sitting towards the back of the bottom deck and looking out of the window when the bus came to a bone-jolting stop. Horns blared furiously, and she craned to see what they'd almost smashed into. She had a moment's glimpse of something shiny and sporty and black driving away, before the bus set off again, the moment over.

Suddenly, she was on edge. She took a long, deep breath, trying to distract herself from subtle fears. The window showed a clean, crisp spring morning, tree-lined streets, empty parks – people waiting at bus stops, hurrying into tube stations, beginning the day. *I'm one of them now*, she thought. *I live here now.*

It surprised her to realise it was true; she'd only been in the capital for two days. She'd been shown round the shared house yesterday afternoon, would move in properly within the next hour. The single suitcase she'd brought with her was the only one in the luggage rack by the bus doors. She kept forgetting about it, then remembering sharply, her eyes darting over to it with a small-town girl's paranoia as she remembered there were thieves in London.

But those moments of panic weren't just about the suitcase. They expressed something far bigger, that she'd never really known before; half exhilarating, half terrifying, a sense of her life as something portable.

Think of the good things, she told herself: *freedom, opportunity.* Around her, she saw life on a different scale from the town she'd grown up in: taller buildings, wider streets and an atmosphere that was hard to put a name to. It was in the eyes and faces and movement of the people she observed – the harassed-looking young man in the baggy suit, the grey-haired woman trailing an ebullient mongrel – an urban look, anonymous. The streets in Underlyme had felt like an extension of home; those around her belonged to nobody.

There's a future here, she told herself, *you can feel alive again;* but deep inside, she was aware that she was keeping her thoughts away from the For Sale sign in front of the house on Acacia Avenue, the memories of twenty-five years rinsed out as carelessly as coffee dregs.

Then the bus was pulling up outside Camden station and she was getting her suitcase, heading out into the morning.

3

BHN Advertising was based in Farringdon, a half-dream, half-nightmare of modern architecture and dark-blue glass. The sunlight reflected off it with a savage glitter as Rachel walked towards it from her now-parked car, still jittery from her brush with death fifteen minutes ago. It was almost half past eight.

Up the curving white-stone steps and through the revolving doors, the building's glamour faded slightly – the fake marble walls and flooring, the suspiciously opulent banks of greenery all trying a little too hard to sustain the façade of elegance. Rachel nodded and smiled at the girl behind the reception desk, before heading over to the lifts.

Out at the fifth floor, striplights buzzed endlessly, merging with the steady hum of the air-con. Rachel crossed the empty open-plan office to her desk, and turned her computer on. Beside it, a leather-framed photograph of herself and Andrew smiled out, caught for posterity at his parents' house last Christmas.

It caught her attention this morning, as it did surprisingly often. She took a mental step back to look at it through a stranger's eyes. The tall, sandy-blond young man with the infinitely reassuring smile, one arm round the thin, attractive young woman with the straight dark hair in a shoulder-length bob. The glint of lavish garlands behind them, the merest suggestion of slanting oak beams . . .

9

Then she heard the door opening across the office, and tore her gaze away as if afraid it might betray something.

'Morning, Rach,' said Kate, as she approached. 'Still on a high about the Fanta pitch?'

'Well, ish.' Rachel smiled, shrugging, embarrassed by her own pride. 'No more than anyone else.'

'You should be. From what I've heard, you had a hell of a lot to do with us winning it.' The big, untidy redhead perched on the edge of Rachel's desk. 'You take Andrew out to celebrate last night?'

'God, no. He thinks I'm obsessed with work as it is. I just told him we'd won Fanta. We stayed in and cooked together.'

'That sounds nice.' Kate looked at her closely. 'Must feel more couply now you're living together – how long's it been now?'

'A month and two weeks.' Rachel's gaze strayed to the photo again, to Andrew's face. 'Feels like years, in a funny sort of way.'

'Is that good or bad?' A brief pause as Rachel laughed an affirmative, then Kate's cosy, big-sisterly expression turned to one of frank curiosity. 'By the way, I'm not being nosy, but what was Diane saying to you yesterday afternoon? You guys were talking for yonks.'

'Oh, just chewing the fat. Doing a little post-mortem on the pitch.' She didn't want to mention the rest to Kate – only the euphoria of yesterday evening had made her mention it to Andrew – but suddenly she found she couldn't help herself. 'She's invited me to lunch.'

'Jesus H. That sounds promising,' said Kate amiably. 'Well, good luck.'

When Kate had gone to her own desk across the room, Rachel checked through her e-mail, wondering over and over what Diane wanted to say to her. A wild optimism trembled in her mind. Beyond the windows, the morning was beautiful.

4

Eleven-thirty in the morning, and Sophie was sitting in a pleasant little café that smelt reassuringly of soup, drinking a Diet Coke by the window, watching people come and go. It had taken her next to no time to unpack, and all but one of her new housemates had been at work. The exception, a small, mousy girl named Leila, was off work with a bad cold, and had welcomed her red-nosed and dressing-gowned, keeping an apologetic distance before shuffling back off to bed. Wandering round the quiet house after unpacking, Sophie had been gripped by a sudden urge to explore the area. She'd walked and walked, enthralled by novelty on all sides before realising how far she'd come; she was tired, her feet hurt a little, the café across the road had beckoned invitingly.

Now, she sat and sipped while time slipped past around her, feeling like a sports car revving up at a red light, intent on the future.

I'll start going round the recruitment agencies tomorrow, she thought. Even though she hadn't consciously been looking, she seemed to have passed dozens of them in the course of her walk here – windows promising secretarial and PA work with good rates of pay. More than ever, the city around her felt alive with opportunity. It was what had brought her here, a premonition of this feeling; with the end of home, she'd had a mounting, ultimately irresistible longing to make a fresh start, to reinvent herself in a place where the past could be forgotten.

She could never have been free of it in Underlyme, Dorset – that deceptively large seaside town with its summer tourists, amusement arcades and crowded town centre, its prejudices and certainties and familiarity. In Underlyme, she saw the same faces everywhere she looked, walking past Next, behind a till in the local newsagent, on the bus home from work. She supposed it wasn't surprising that she knew so many people, when she'd lived in the same place all her life. Still, as the last few months had unwound, she'd found herself longing for anonymity like fresh air; found herself thinking there was nothing left to keep her there.

And now, here she was. In Camden . . .

Sitting by the window, she remembered her mother's voice in the kitchen back home, last April. *I saw Nina in town. We stopped for a chat,* she'd said. *I hear Rachel's doing well, she's living in Camden now.* At the time, it hadn't meant anything much, had just been a source of vague and fleeting interest. But when she'd been flicking through the Accommodation section of *London Loot* the day before yesterday, the place-name had come back to her out of the blue. *Shared house in Camden,* she'd read, and the last word had got bigger second by second; she'd experienced a nameless fascination, maddening as an unreachable itch.

To think Rachel was alive in the world at this exact moment; Sophie had been driven towards the particular house by a disinterested longing to run into her again, to know what had happened to her and how she was. *Doing well* answered none of the questions that gnawed away in her mind, and as she'd thought about them, she'd experienced something like a physical hunger for answers.

But now she was here, the area seemed vast. Even walking to this café, she'd seemed to see a thousand doors behind which Rachel could be living; a million different routes she could take to the tube station; an infinity of ways they could co-exist in this area for ten years and never see each other once. The idea of a chance encounter had begun to look flimsy and implausible, and it embarrassed her that she'd been so convinced it would happen here.

Still, it didn't matter. It wasn't why she'd come to this city. Finding a job would be easier here, she thought; everything would be easier. As she sat and looked out of the window, the sun appeared from behind a cloud. The sudden glint of light on the glass obscured the view for a second, and she glimpsed her own reflection: dark-blonde hair, slight build, hazel eyes untouched by experience – a woman of twenty-five who looked seventeen, impatient for life to begin.

5

Diane Robinson was a small, plump, glamorous blonde in her mid-forties, with inch-long French-manicured nails, and the voice and manner of a soap-opera barmaid. Rumour had it that she was a world-class bitch, but Rachel thought that was mostly jealous bullshit; she hadn't had much to do with the Senior Account Director thus far in her career, but so far, Diane seemed okay.

They were sitting at a window table in an elegant, modern little restaurant near the office, and the waiter was taking their order. 'The Caesar salad looks good,' said Rachel. 'Think I'll go for that. Forget the diet today.'

Diane laughed; a harsh, bawdy echo of the Queen Vic rang out sharply against the background noise, the clink of cutlery on plates, the steady murmur of other people's lunchtime conversations. 'Think I'll go for the same,' she said, then leaned closer to Rachel across the table. 'But seriously, well done on that Fanta pitch, Rach. You had a hell of a lot to do with us getting it. I know that.'

Rachel couldn't think of anything to say; it was true, but the last thing she wanted was to sound cocky. 'I loved working on it,' she said at last. 'I'm just glad it went so well.'

'It's the first major pitch you've worked on with us, isn't it?'

Rachel nodded, watched Diane watching her over the table. Diane's eyes were pale and piercing, as out of place with her brash façade as a Roedean education would have been. 'How long you been in this industry now?' she asked. 'Four years?'

'Five. I was at Markson Vickery for two, as a graduate trainee. Then I moved here.'

'Making you how old?'

The signs were getting better and better – Diane spoke with frank interest, as if she wanted to get to know her. They'd never talked about anything that wasn't work before. 'Twenty-six,' said Rachel. 'Last month.'

'Well, you're doing dead well for your age.' Diane was matey, expansive, encouraging. 'Here comes the bloke again – fancy a glass of wine?'

'Oh – no thanks,' said Rachel quickly. 'This water's fine.'

'Well – if you're sure.' Diane stopped the waiter. 'I'll have a glass of Chardonnay,' she said brusquely, before returning her full attention to Rachel. 'I'm going to be putting in a good word for you at the next senior management meeting, Rach. I reckon you're ready to take on a lot more responsibility – don't you?'

While the word *promotion* hadn't been specifically mentioned, Rachel suddenly knew for a fact that this was what this lunch was about. She'd have had to be deaf and blind not to: the nuances of Diane's voice, the conspiratorial look in those pale eyes. It was a struggle to keep her own voice steady, unruffled. 'I'd like to think so.'

'We'll see what we can do. Of course, I can't promise anything – but I'm going to do my best. I'm bloody impressed with you, Rach. You know it.'

Their food arrived; Diane picked up her cutlery and started eating. Rachel followed suit. The conversation didn't grind to a halt; they discussed events at Brent Harvey Nash, a recent movie, a high-profile sex scandal in the news. But Rachel was well aware that this part of lunch was like the closing credits of a movie, and that the main feature was over and done.

'Well,' said Diane at last, 'suppose we'd better be getting back.' Then they were heading out and beginning the five-minute walk back to the office, Rachel's mind spinning with the future of her dreams; ultimate security and prestige suddenly seeming close enough to touch.

6

Working as he did for a major investment bank in the City, Andrew often didn't finish till late. When Rachel's key turned in the lock, it was seven thirty and getting dark. The flat was silent apart from the phone ringing in the hallway. She flicked the light on and went to get it.

'Hi, Rachel. It's me.'

'Mum – how are you?'

'All right, thanks. Got back from the shop an hour or so ago. Another hard day of weighing up yoghurt-coated pineapple chunks and God knows what.' Down the line, Nina Carter laughed. 'Can't believe I've been there five years now. I'm not even that keen on health food.'

'I thought you liked the job.'

'Oh, it's okay. I like the people, it pays the rent. You know I've never been ambitious like you – even when I was young.'

These days, Rachel never quite relaxed as she did with Nina. It changed her whole posture, the look in her eyes. If Andrew had been in the flat, she would have been self-conscious about it. 'You're still young,' she said, 'well, young-ish. You're not forty-one yet.'

'Don't remind me.' A theatrical groan. 'By the way, I've been wondering all day. How did that lunch with your boss go?'

'Well . . .' With anyone else she would have been edgy and evasive, but she hadn't hidden anything from Nina in years. 'I'm quite excited, to be honest. She was dropping some heavy hints about promotion. Seems to really think I'm ready for it.'

'Oh, Rachel. That's fantastic.' A brief pause fell. 'I can't get over how well you're doing these days, just like when you were a kid. When I look back to – you know, all that happened, it's like thinking about a different person.'

It shrivelled Rachel like a bucket of cold water. Her whole demeanour changed, a snail drawing back into its shell. 'That was a long time ago,' she said. 'Anyway, Mum, I'd better make a start on dinner. I'm cooking tonight.'

'Oh – if you must.' Nina spoke blithely. 'Give my love to Andrew.'

Off the phone, Rachel went into the kitchen and got the ingredients of a chicken casserole out of the fridge. Despite herself, she felt shaken. She loved Nina's thinly veiled pride in her success, as she had done as a child; the straight As and the chance of promotion, the much-loved, all-achieving girl who always got everything right. But equally, she hated it when Nina referred to that other time, those dark and tangled secret years she'd never really understood. The casual way Nina spoke about it, as if the passage of time and achievement somehow drained it of horror. It was why she always felt so uncomfortable when Nina and Andrew were in the same place, why she tried to keep them apart as much as she could. The idea that, in a casual remark, Nina might reveal—

Of course, deep down she knew Nina wouldn't tell him in a million years. Her unease when they were together was instinctive, irrational. There were too many things that she and Nina knew, the knowledge sinister beside Andrew's unsuspecting openness; a too-long silence when certain subjects came up in conversation, a too-quick change of subject. Nina had no talent for subterfuge whatsoever, and on the rare occasions they'd all been together, Rachel had sensed Andrew's occasional puzzlement.

Still, if he had noticed anything, he'd never mentioned it to her afterwards. And she knew that he'd never come close to guessing the truth. Even Nina didn't know all of it. Only one other person in the world did, and Rachel had left her far behind, long ago.

Back in Underlyme . . .

The thought soothed her. She put the radio on and carried on preparing the dinner, blocking out unwelcome memories, waiting for Andrew to come home.

7

'So what are you up to this weekend?'

It was half eleven, and the office was surprisingly quiet for a Friday. Kate had come over to Rachel's desk and was perched on it as usual, drinking a plastic cup of coffee from the machine. Rachel glanced at the photo by her computer.

'Nothing earth-shattering,' she said. 'We're off to see Andrew's sister tonight. She's supposed to be cooking but I don't hold out much hope – she's too young to be Delia Smith yet. She's only just finished her A levels.'

'What is it? Family reunion or something?'

'Oh, no. Just business, in a way. She's off travelling soon, taking a gap year before uni. So a very nice flat's going to be pretty much empty all that time.'

Kate's eyebrows rose. 'Come again?'

'Andrew's folks live in Oxford, but they've got a pad in Fulham too. Andrew used to live there, but when we decided to move in together, we wanted somewhere bigger, and didn't want the whole clan marching in whenever they were in town.' *The whole clan* – the words warmed her; she carried on, smiling. 'His dad uses it about twice a year, when he stays in London on business. And his sister's been living there for the last few weeks.'

'So what are you planning to do? Put it on the market?'

'God, no. Andrew's folks would go crazy. But he's hoping we can let it out, at least while his sister's away. His dad can stay in a hotel. And the money would come in useful.'

'Bet it would.' A faint muted ringing began across the room, and Kate hopped off Rachel's desk, nearly spilling her coffee. 'Shit, that's my phone. Better get back to work, eh?'

Nobody who worked above a certain level at BHN had to go out for lunch unless they wanted to – free food from Pret à Manger was a perk of the job. The rangy young man who took the orders was coming round now. Rachel watched him from the corner of her eye as she always did, feeling something strange in the air between them, wildly out of proportion to the situation itself.

'Hi, Peter,' she said. 'How's it going?'

He looked at her for a long second. 'I'm all right. You?'

'Same old same old.' She always found herself hugging normality during these brief exchanges, clichés she habitually disliked and avoided. 'Thank God it's Friday.'

As always, she had an unplaceable feeling he saw too much. He nodded, half smiling, and silence extended between them. 'Do you want anything?' he asked at last. 'From Pret?'

'Sushi, please. And a bag of vegetable chips.'

He nodded, wrote briefly on his order form, turned away. Again, Rachel found herself watching him. She didn't like to acknowledge it in her own mind, but the sight of him brought an uneasy, squirming fascination – an echo of herself from all those years ago, the self she'd struggled to escape from . . .

Then she brushed him deliberately from her thoughts and got back to work, thinking of half five, the end of the week, dinner with Helen.

8

The time was almost one o'clock when Sophie turned the corner and saw the City Slickers agency come into sight. She'd seen the ad for it in the *Evening Standard* yesterday, and it had caught her attention; colourful, friendly, full of promise. As she came closer, she realised it looked exactly as she'd expected. Around her, Covent Garden was bustling, intent on the afternoon's business.

She stepped in, trying to project an aura of efficiency, comforted and reassured by knowledge of her own neatness – skirt suit, white blouse, hair tied back in a French plait. She'd spent a long time preparing for this interview, back in

Camden. 'Excuse me,' she said, approaching the receptionist, 'I've got an appointment at one with Vanessa. I phoned yesterday – my name's Sophie Townsend.'

'If you'll just take a seat, I'll let her know you're here.'

Sophie sat. It seemed no time at all till a young woman with a bright, efficient smile was approaching her through the reception area. 'Sophie? I'm Vanessa. If you'd like to come through.'

Sophie followed Vanessa through a big sunny office, sat down across from her at a desk. 'Did you find us okay?' Vanessa asked, still smiling.

'Oh, yes, thanks. Just followed your directions from the tube station.'

Around her, Sophie heard ringing telephones being answered, keyboards being busily tapped at. The atmosphere was all youth and vitality, an overwhelming sense of work as fun. 'So,' said Vanessa, 'you're interested in temping work?'

'Definitely. I think it sounds really interesting.'

'Of course, you've got experience.'

'Oh, yes. I moved here from Dorset last week. I've been an admin assistant there for years.'

The bright smile stayed on, but something cooled five degrees in the eyes. 'I meant specific secretarial experience. Admin isn't *quite* the same.'

It was like a rug being pulled away from under Sophie's feet. She struggled to keep her balance, not to show her dismay. 'Well, I was looking for a change, really,' she said quickly. 'I've got general office skills – I can fax, I can e-mail.'

'You're used to Powerpoint?' Sophie shook her head. 'Excel? Spreadsheets?'

More than anything, Sophie wanted to say yes, but couldn't. 'I'm forty words a minute typing. I'm sure I could learn all the rest in no time.'

'I'm sure you could.' The smile was gone now. Vanessa's face was earnest, not unkind, but slightly patronising. 'But our clients want people with experience, I'm afraid. I've never heard of a temp getting on-the-job training.'

Sophie sat and looked at her across the desk for a second. It was as if a gulf had opened between them, the atmosphere had changed beyond expression. She didn't want to ask, but forced herself to. 'So you don't think I'm experienced enough for temp work?'

'I'm really sorry.' Vanessa paused; Sophie was barely aware of the noise around her. 'If I was you, I'd keep an eye out for another admin job. There must be loads around, and you don't need to go through an agency for one of those. Just look at the ads in your local paper.'

'All right,' Sophie heard herself saying. 'I'll do that.'

'Well, I hope you find something that's right for you. I'm sorry we couldn't be more help.'

'Oh, no. Thanks, really.' A moment of awkwardness, then Sophie rose from her seat. 'Thanks a lot for your time,' she said again, and then she was leaving, past the desks, through the office noise, into reception, where she smiled a goodbye at the girl on the desk, joyless as an apology.

Outside, she headed back to the tube station, full of an inner numbness. It had never occurred to her that finding a better job might be impossible here, that they'd ask for skills and experience she didn't have. As if a cloud had passed across the sun, she felt the world changing around her; open doors closing in her face as she watched.

9

Rachel liked Andrew's whole family, but was particularly fond of Helen. When they'd first met, Helen had irresistibly reminded her of someone else – small and slight, with dark-blonde hair and hazel eyes, a delicate and slightly ethereal prettiness. But the more she'd seen of Helen, the less that likeness had bothered her. Her company was as pleasant and undemanding as a warm bath, and the easy brightness of her life seemed contagious.

'Hi,' she said in the doorway. 'Come on in.'

Rachel and Andrew followed her into the spacious, well-decorated Fulham flat. Helen's three-week sojourn showed in messiness entirely devoid of squalor – a kind of cheerful, laid-back chaos, implying too many exciting things going on at once, and not enough time to tidy up. 'Sorry it's a bit of a pigsty,' Helen apologised, as they came into the kitchen. 'I'd have cleaned up earlier, but I've been tied up all day, making my final list of the stuff I'll need to take with me.'

Andrew watched her with amused exasperation. 'I thought you made your final list last week?'

'That turned out to be a sort of semi-final list. I'd have needed about eight backpacks to fit all *that* in.' Helen smiled. 'Now I'm trying to get it down to the things I'll really need.'

'The bare necessities of life,' said Andrew. They all sat down at the kitchen table, and he pretended to count off on his fingers. 'Hairdryer, hot rollers, shower spray, dressing table – have I left something out?'

'Oh, ha ha. I don't know how you put up with him sometimes, Rachel.' Helen turned back to her brother. 'What do you know about travelling anyway?'

'Book time off work at least a month in advance. And make sure your hotel's already been built.' Andrew grinned, shrugged. 'Sorry, Helen, but the hippy trail's never really appealed. I like novelty, but I like an easy life more.'

'Nothing *too* foreign,' said Rachel drily. 'Nothing you can't put an English name to.'

'A born tourist,' said Helen, with the airy disdain of the seasoned traveller. 'Oh, by the way, bad news. I spoke to Dad this morning. He's dead set against getting a lodger for this place.'

Andrew groaned. 'Should have seen *that* coming. Let me guess – he likes staying here when he's in town, and hotels always feel so depressing.'

'And anonymous. And sterile. And make him feel like a travelling salesman selling vacuum cleaners.' Helen shrugged helplessly. 'You know Dad. He's just a wee bit set in his ways.'

'Oh, don't I know it. What the hell, it was just an idea.' Andrew's eyes moved suspiciously around the kitchen's bare surfaces and unemployed cooker. 'Don't mean to be rude, Hel, but any danger of something edible? Rachel and I are about to starve to death here.'

'Don't worry. I called up the pizza place before you got here. We'll have something on the table in about fifteen mins.' Helen jumped up from her seat. 'And I've got some wine, too. I'll crack it open.'

'We'll make a dinner party hostess of you yet,' said Andrew, getting up. 'Just off to the loo. Back in a minute.'

Helen got the bottle out of the fridge. Seeing her taking three glasses from a cupboard, Rachel cut in quickly. 'None for me, thanks.'

'Sorry. I *always* forget – I'll get you some apple juice.' Helen looked at her closely. 'You know, I don't think I ever met a real live teetotaller before you. Is it a health thing or something?'

'Oh, nothing like that. Just don't like the taste.' Seeing Helen's gaze fixed on her across the kitchen, Rachel felt a wave of unease. 'Never have,' she said, and watched Helen pour two glasses of wine, trying to find a way of changing the subject before Andrew came back into the room.

10

The time was ticking past nine o'clock, and Sophie was sitting at the desk in her room, going over the paper she'd bought that afternoon. Wondering if she'd maybe missed something, even as dispiriting words told her she hadn't. *Filing, typing, answering the phone. Two days a week, five pounds an hour. Experience essential.*

Over the past week, she'd visited four other recruitment

agencies. They'd all told her exactly what City Slickers had, only, in one case, less politely. She remembered a severe-looking middle-aged woman fixing her with a cold stare across a desk yesterday afternoon. *I have to tell you, you're just wasting your time looking for this kind of work. Your CV simply isn't up to scratch.* The memory made her cheeks burn even now, driving home the incredible, painful arrogance of her initial naivety. She'd honestly thought that she'd walk into a better job as easily as through an open door . . .

She scanned the employers who were advertising in today's Admin section: a solicitor's office in Brixton, a local authority in Essex, the clerical office of a paper factory in Luton. It was a million miles from the wild dreams that had brought her here. She found it too easy to imagine those places, to quick-sketch a mental picture from the years she'd spent in Underlyme Council's admin department. Chipped coffee mugs and grey filing cabinets, ancient computers and institutional clocks whose seconds ticked out too slowly – an office full of dour thirty-something women who'd never have dreamed of socialising after work. A working life like a prison sentence. She had no idea how she'd managed to waste all those years like that, but now that she had done, she was troubled by a mounting suspicion that she'd left it too late to escape.

And how she longed for a new start, to somehow rediscover the fearlessness and easy joy of all those years ago. Before the summer holiday when it had all changed, back when the world had been friendly – before she'd had to learn about secrecy and fear—

You're lying! she remembered, and shivered involuntarily, turning away from the memory.

At least she'd had some friends in Underlyme. They'd thought she was insane to come here, to a place she'd never been before in her life. She pushed the newspaper to one side, beginning to agree with them for the first time. The others in the house were almost always out in the evenings, and their lives seemed barely to touch one another, aside from rushed exchanges in the hallway. *I'll give it another fortnight,* she thought, *just another fortnight, then I'll admit this was all a mistake.* Part of her was packing her suitcase even now, buying an adult single ticket, checking the flickering boards at Waterloo for the time of the next train to Underlyme.

11

On Sunday morning, Andrew came into the kitchen, casually dressed, swinging his sports bag over one shoulder. 'Well, better be off,' he said. 'Don't want to keep poor old Tim waiting before I thrash him.'

She heard the front door close behind him. As often, the depth of her affection took her by surprise. He played squash with his friend Tim every Sunday afternoon. It didn't mean anything, but somehow it seemed to epitomise everything about him she'd fallen in love with. Small, comfortable rituals and an overwhelming sense of stability; inherent sociability, easy friendships that dated back to childhood. So comfortable with the world and his place in it, so unafraid of anything. Not an ostentatious fearlessness, but something as natural to him as breathing.

She remembered the first time he'd taken her to meet his parents, when they'd been seeing each other for maybe three months. The senior Megsons had a beautiful home in a semi-rural stockbroker belt, but it hadn't been the gleaming oak panels and gilt-framed paintings that had seduced her. Rather, it had been the openness of it all, the way everything was offered to the visitor as casually as a box of chocolates. The parents like two halves of the same unit, apparently married since the dawn of time itself – they finished each other's jokes and teased each other with the ease of long-term friends, as comfortable with one another as they were in their own skins.

Andrew and I could be like that, one day – the thought had brought the greatest longing of her life, and in the Megsons' living room she'd been momentarily weak with it. Perhaps it was that afternoon which had put the final seal on her love for him. Then and there, she'd known that she'd never feel like this about any man again, as long as she lived. She yearned to be part of his life, with its absolute lack of secrecy . . .

Abruptly, her thoughts turned to the young man named Peter at work. The juxtaposition jolted her, and she forced him from her mind.

The flat often felt strange when Andrew was out on Sundays, but the unusual brightness of today underlined that feeling – the elegance around her somehow alien, the absence of voices making the radio too clear, too loud. As she hoovered the rooms, the flat whine seeming to echo, she was gripped by a sudden yearning restlessness. It wasn't a day to spend alone at home; it was a day to go for a stroll, wander through Camden Market, maybe have a cappuccino by the window of a pleasant café, reading the Sunday paper, watching the people come and go. And suddenly, she wanted it so badly that it was an effort to finish vacuuming the bedroom, to put the hoover back in the wardrobe of the spare room, to put on light touches of make-up and perfume before getting her handbag and walking out into the day.

12

Sophie sat in the Camden café that she'd discovered on her first day of living here, and had visited on an occasional basis ever since. The scene she saw through the window could have been cut straight out of her Underlyme dreams – crowds and laughter and infinite human variety, hippies and Goths and Rastafarians, trendy teenagers and students with backpacks, all spilling into the entrance to Camden Market across the road.

She observed it with a wistful kind of envy, as if she saw it all on a TV screen. More than ever before, she felt herself belonging to Underlyme. She was relieved to observe another woman coming in on her own, sitting down at the next table. Solitude had begun to feel like her own exclusive burden.

And there could be no real stigma in that solitude, if the woman at the next table shared it. At first, Sophie glanced casually, then with a kind of fascination; the deceptively careless curve of the woman's dark bob, the stylish little tan leather handbag, the air of casual, independent urban affluence she seemed to carry with her. The way she unfolded her paper and started reading, indifferent to solitude as only those accustomed to company could be. Watching her covertly, Sophie felt gauche and naive and suburban. The casual word to the approaching waitress, the quick businesslike smile, the birdlike tilt of the head as she returned her attention to the front page—

In that split second, Sophie's vague interest snapped into something else. Something about that tilt of the head struck a random note in a silent part of her mind, and she was suddenly aware of other things. The thin, high-cheekboned, rather nervy attractiveness, a streak of sunlight catching red on the straight dark hair. An androgynous, elegant quality that had always seemed out of place back in Underlyme, that instantly reminded Sophie of—

a long hot summer in Acacia Avenue. Two girls in the garden. Tears and revelation and glacial rejection masquerading as hysteria – rejection that had resonated down the years of Sophie's life, echoes growing louder as time passed—

You're lying!

—and told her that this was the chance meeting that she'd come to Camden in search of, that she'd written off as an impossible dream only days ago.

She'd thought she wanted this moment, but she'd never imagined how awkward it would feel. For a second, she had no idea what to do. She could turn and hurry out, driving away the truth of recognition and the dark secrets it carried in its wake, or she could approach, force a melodramatic confrontation that might or might not end with forgiveness. But convention proved stronger than cowardice or bravery. Seeing that Rachel had seen and recognised her too, she felt the bright school-reunion smile on her lips; watched Rachel's own identical greeting, heard her call out across the room.

'Sophie?'

13

They'd last seen each other eight years ago, on a Saturday afternoon in October, in Underlyme's crowded town centre. Coming out of Top Shop on the outskirts of a noisy teenage group, she'd seen Rachel walking in the centre of another. Their eyes had met across the street, and a brief electric moment of unease and subtle hatred had flashed between them; both had walked on without speaking. Impossible to think they'd been best friends, once.

But as Rachel came over, Sophie's moment of horror was eclipsed by inexplicable delight – a familiar face in a strange land, someone who knew the same landscapes, spoke the same language. The waitress came with Rachel's coffee, saw she'd moved tables and brought it over.

'I don't believe it,' Rachel said, taking the coffee with a quick, distracted smile. 'This can't be happening. It's like a movie.'

Sophie was startled by this apparently mutual joy in recognition – looking across the table, she tried not to let her amazement show. She remembered all the things that had happened to Rachel in the aftermath of that fateful summer, the terrible things she'd heard about through the grapevine of St Andrews' Secondary. Realised what she'd felt but never consciously recognised back then. *Well, that's her finished.* As spring preceded summer, teenage years like that preceded a life of substance abuse, homelessness, social workers; it was the inevitable conclusion, whatever Nina had said about her doing well.

Now, she looked across the table at the elegant young woman she'd admired before recognising, and told herself her own surprise held no trace of jealousy.

'So how's life been treating you?' Rachel went on. 'When did you move here?'

'Just the week before last. It's all sort of new to me.'

Rachel watched her intently. 'Where were you before?'

'Oh – well, Underlyme.'

'My God. All this time?' Sophie nodded. 'Still living at home, or . . . ?'

Her words tailed off, and Sophie had an overwhelming sense of strangeness; a garden in Acacia Avenue summoned up and shimmering like a heat haze between them. 'I never quite got round to moving out,' she said. 'But Dad died the year before last in a car crash, and now Mum's married again. I couldn't live with her and her new bloke.'

Silence fell – Sophie's eyes danced nervously round the café, to the counter, the next table, the window. She didn't want to see the new, guarded tension in Rachel's expression, have to guess at what Rachel was thinking right now. She wanted to get this conversation as far away from Underlyme as possible.

'But anyway, that's all water under the bridge,' she said lamely. 'Tell me about you. What are you doing for a living these days?'

'Account manager at an advertising agency. Sounds more impressive than it is, believe me. There's about twenty-five of us.' At first Rachel spoke lightly, then more seriously, lowering her voice. 'State secret, but I'm hoping to make it to senior account manager soon. Looks like promotion might be on the cards.'

'Wow, Rachel.' Even Rachel's way of speaking had changed, she thought – snappier, more confident, more *together*. She had to remind herself what the old Rachel had been like, to hold awe at bay. 'At your age – that's fantastic.'

'Oh, the whole agency's doing well. They're taking on new

people all over the place – winning a lot of new business, you know how it is.' Rachel smiled a quick, professional little smile, shrugged modestly before carrying on. 'So how's your love life? Seeing anyone back in Underlyme?'

'Not really.' Sensing her words implied too much, she wanted to mitigate them, but there seemed no way of doing so. The weight of morbid mutual curiosity was strong between them; she sensed they were both wondering what scars remained on the other from a summer nearly fourteen years ago. 'What about you? Are you going out with anyone?'

'Living together now.' An underlying triumph in Rachel's voice, like pulling back cloth to reveal smooth, unmarked skin. 'Best decision I ever made. Never been happier.'

'What's he like? Your boyfriend?'

'Name's Andrew. Works in the City.' Rachel reached into her handbag, fished out and opened her wallet. 'That's him.'

Rachel flashed the neat interior of tan leather and credit cards. A pleasant-faced young man with sandy-blond hair smiled out from behind a plastic panel. 'Oh, Rachel. He looks really nice,' said Sophie.

'He's terrific.' The wallet was closed, refastened, replaced; Rachel checked her watch. To Sophie, the gesture seemed subtly pointed. 'Christ, look at the time. I'm sorry, but I've got to run.'

'Well, it's been nice catching up.' It felt like last orders being called on a night that was just getting into its stride. Sophie felt a ridiculously profound disappointment. 'I'll give you my mobile number, if you like. We could meet up again some time.'

'Tell you what, I'll give you my card.' Out came the wallet again – a moment's glimpse of the nice-looking blond man before Rachel's card was passed across the table. 'Call me sometime,' Rachel said. 'Whenever.'

An offhand gesture across the café, and the waitress was there with a bill for the two of them. Rachel handed over a ten-pound note. 'No worries,' she said, as Sophie tried to join in. 'It's on me.'

Outside, in the chilly sunlight, they walked together for a few minutes before Rachel stopped. 'Here's where I leave you. Great seeing you again.' She air-kissed Sophie twice, lips just missing each cheek in a gesture Sophie knew from movies rather than life. 'Bye.'

'Bye, Rachel,' said Sophie. 'I'll call you at work sometime.'

She stood for a second and watched Rachel walking away, remembering the teenager she'd known. She wondered if the sandy-blond boyfriend in the wallet knew about all that, and if so, how on earth he'd reacted.

Then Rachel disappeared round a corner, and was gone.

14

'Well, it's happening, Rach,' said Diane. 'You're being promoted.'

Part of her had known the second Diane had invited her in, but still, for a second, she couldn't think of a single thing to say. 'God,' she said quietly, at last. 'That's great.'

'There was a management meeting after work on Friday. I put in a word for you there – well, quite a few, as it happens. Nothing against you, Rach, but some of the others didn't think you had quite enough experience yet.' A smile of conspiratorial reassurance across the desk, the pale eyes shrewder than ever. 'I managed to talk them round. I've got every confidence in you, like I said when we went out for lunch. I know you can handle it.'

'Thanks.' She struggled to project the right image, calmly pleased, self-assured, fighting back a fierce delight that could easily be seen as unprofessional. 'You won't regret it.'

'I'll announce it over the e-mail this afternoon. You'll get a letter through the internal mail, telling you all the private-and-confidential stuff – pay, benefits, you know the sort of thing. And you'll have Gavin's old office. You can move in first thing tomorrow, when the computer's set up.' A long pause, dizzy with the weight of longed-for news. 'Well, what do you think?' Diane asked at last. 'Happy?'

'Very,' said Rachel, then, scared she'd do or say something childish and impulsive, she rose from her seat, smoothing her skirt down. 'You just made my day, Diane.'

She left Diane's office, walked past Kate's desk and over to her own. Almost instantly, Kate found an excuse to walk to the printer across the room, stopping off at Rachel's desk on the way back. 'Well?' she murmured, leaning over as if to read off her computer screen. 'Was that little meeting just now what I think it was?'

'Yes.' Kate seemed about to exclaim aloud, and Rachel spoke quickly. 'But it's not going public till later.'

'Say no more – not a word. But congrats.' The attempts at subtle diplomacy were as arrestingly inept as an elephant ballet-dancing; the too-audible whisper, the broad, sidelong wink. 'Fancy going for a *confidential* lunch later? You must want to celebrate.'

'I'd love to.'

'Say about half twelve-ish?'

Rachel nodded. As Kate returned to her desk, she picked up the phone, dialling Andrew's direct line. 'Great news.' She spoke quietly into the receiver, almost whispering. 'Guess who just got promoted?'

'Bloody hell – congratulations! Let's go and celebrate up West tonight. The boys can do without me for one night – might even remember the rules.'

Another of his rituals, the Monday-night poker game. 'I've got a better idea. Let's stay in,' she said. 'Oh, I just remembered. We're almost out of olive oil. I'll stop off and get some on the way home.'

'Heaven forbid we should celebrate without it.' He laughed. 'See you tonight, sweetheart. Well done.'

The rest of Monday morning passed quickly. At lunchtime, she and Kate headed for the lift. When it finally arrived, the doors opened to reveal the young man named Peter. He and

Rachel nodded a strange, terse greeting to each other before he walked away.

She said, half to herself, 'I wonder what he does when he's not here.'

'Who cares?' Kate shrugged, looked at her closely. 'You often talk about him. What's so interesting about him anyway?'

'Oh, nothing.' She felt oddly uneasy that her interest had been noticed, as if she'd been caught reading *Mein Kampf* or the Marquis de Sade. She hurried to change the subect. 'I just can't believe it,' she said, lowering her voice. 'From what Diane said, she really went out of her way to get me promoted.'

'Well, maybe.' For a second, Kate looked frankly sceptical. 'But I bet she didn't do it out of the kindness of her heart.'

'How do you mean?'

'It's going to look bloody good for her, isn't it? When you start winning the big accounts, she can say, if it wasn't for me, the great Rachel Carter might have moved on to AMV or Saatchi's. It was me who knew she was ready for it, it was me who gave her the chance.' As they came out into the sunshine, Kate grinned. 'Okay, tell me I'm a cynic.'

'No – you're probably right,' Rachel admitted. 'I know she's not exactly a philanthropist.'

'That's the understatement of the twenty-first century. She got Gavin fired for missing a deadline, so I heard,' said Kate. 'Still, if you say she's all right . . .' And they walked on to Pizza Express, for a pleasant, gossipy lunch.

When they got back, the internal letter Diane had mentioned was on Rachel's desk. She sat down, tore it open and skimmed feverishly; delight swept over her when she came to the salary figure. It was really happening, she realised. It was what she'd dreamed of.

15

'Well done on your promotion, Rachel! You must be really pleased.'

It was the end of the day, and she was in the lift with two account managers she vaguely knew, Sara and Christina. Their names were inseparable to a point where it was hard to imagine them having different lives outside work. Christina was short, blonde and giggly, invariably dressed in little-girl pastels; Sara had a narrow, foxy face and a lot of shiny red hair, seemed at once nervy and absolutely confident. It had been Sara who'd spoken. 'Thanks,' said Rachel. 'Suppose I am.'

'I couldn't believe it when Diane announced it over the e-mail this afternoon,' said Christina. 'You joined just after we did, didn't you?' Rachel nodded. 'How long were you in advertising before that?'

'Two years at Markson Vickery.' They got out of the lift and walked through the reception area in silence. 'Well,' said Sara outside the revolving doors, 'we're going this way. See you tomorrow.'

'Have a good evening.'

Rachel walked to the side street where she'd parked, telling herself she'd imagined the flicker of jealousy in their eyes. She didn't want anything to spoil this evening's elation. It was almost eight o'clock now, dark and chilly. Getting into the car, she turned on the air-con to warm it up, began the long drive home.

She was ten minutes away from home when she remembered the olive oil. Stopping at a garage, she stepped out into the misty forecourt lights and went into the shop, towards the food section. She was carrying the bottle over to the till when the scenery around her became something more, the drinks section taking on a sudden nightmare clarity in the corner of her eye, reminding her of—

the bottle passing from hand to hand in the shelter on

Underlyme promenade. Late at night. Rain coming down. A sense of life itself collapsing, of terror and hatred and helplessness—

You're lying!

—before the memory snapped off and she was standing under bright shop lights as if momentarily hypnotised. The man behind the till was reading the paper and hadn't noticed her stillness. She paid and left, started the car again and noticed her fingers were trembling as she turned the ignition key.

She hadn't remembered the past that vividly in years – it was because of her chance meeting with Sophie yesterday afternoon, she realised. Of course, she hadn't told Andrew anything about it. The idea of him even knowing Sophie's name brushed a cold steel finger up the back of her neck. *I can't believe I gave her my card*, she thought. *Talk about a Pavlovian reaction. I've been to too many client meetings.* Looking back to that Camden café, she was amazed by her own recollected lack of fear. To talk to someone who knew so many terrible things about you without a flicker of nerves, when all the time, part of you could remember—

But she forced the thought away, hard. She'd talked to Sophie because she had to, because sensible, rational adults weren't scared of the past. But that didn't mean she had to see Sophie again. *If she calls, I'll just say I'm busy till she gives up. We'll never run into each other again, in a city this size.*

Then she was approaching the apartment building and seeing Andrew's sports BMW in the forecourt, hearing Sophie's voice in the back of her mind. *Dad died the year before last in a car crash*, she remembered, and parked in her usual space, forcing herself to focus on the celebrations ahead.

When she let herself in, she could hear muted jazz music coming from the kitchen. Walking quickly through the hallway, she went in. The table was laid for two, replete with blinding white tablecloth, lit candles, flower arrangement. Andrew was standing by the cooker, dressed in jeans and red-striped shirt, adding something to a sizzling frying pan. At the sound of Rachel's footsteps, he turned.

'Looks like I beat you home,' he said.

'Jesus – I wasn't expecting all this!'

'Well, I thought we'd better mark the occasion. You don't get promoted every day. I know it means a lot to you.'

How unbelievably lucky she was to have him. Looking at the scene, Rachel was inexplicably on the brink of tears. She fought them back, not wanting him to see. She'd never cried in front of him. The idea of him seeing her out of control and defenceless was unthinkable.

'Well, it smells delicious,' she said at last, then, sniffing the air, 'Spaghetti bolognese?'

'How did you guess?'

'Must be psychic.' She couldn't help laughing at his surprised expression. 'Come on, it's your party piece. Not that I'm complaining.'

'Should hope not,' he said. 'I'm good at it, admit it.'

'You're great at it. You should set up your own restaurant.'

'Can see the menu now. Spaghetti bolognese. Spaghetti bolognese. Spaghetti bolognese suprise.' He paused for a second, stirring the contents of the frying pan. 'That's spaghetti without spaghetti or bolognese. A sort of china plate thing.'

At the table, they sat and looked at each other; he got up to turn the light off, and the candles gave a soft, rosy, flattering glow. 'Well,' he said, 'bon appetit.'

They ate, discussed her promotion, before the conversation

moved on to Helen's trip. 'I'd better call her before she leaves,' said Rachel. 'I'll ring her from work in the morning.'

When the last plate was dried and stacked away neatly, it was almost half eleven. 'Looks like bedtime,' Andrew said mock-regretfully, then, with a courtly flourish, 'No, you have the bathroom first. I insist.'

As usual, Rachel brushed her teeth, cleansed, toned and moisturised before entering the bedroom. As she set the alarm for the morning, she could hear Andrew washing his face. She got into bed and waited for him with a kind of trepidation. When at last he came in, he joined her in bed and kissed her. She could feel him reaching to turn the bedside light out, and hurried to stop his hand. 'No,' she said. 'Please. Leave it on.'

'Sorry. I always forget that.' He looked at her quizzically. 'You know, I can't work you out sometimes. You're not normally scared of the dark – you can *sleep* with the light out.'

It unsettled her when he said things like that. An image of Sophie rose in her mind like a cork bobbing up in water. 'I know,' she said quickly. 'I don't know why. It's just how I am.' And before he could ask further, she kissed him hard and deep, with a kind of feverish urgency. In her mind, everything descended to a red and thrashing oblivion, a frantic attempt to lose herself in him.

17

The mobile on Sophie's dressing table was whispering to her. But she knew there was no point calling Julie, or Lisa, or Marianne. All her old Underlyme friends would tell her *come home*. Lonely as she was, she didn't want to hear that. Part of her still clung to a belief that there might be something better here, especially since that unexpected meeting with Rachel. Conclusive, living proof that there could be more to life than the grey filing cabinets and council offices, that it was somehow possible to achieve what she wanted to.

It was approaching nine o'clock, and she was sitting at her desk, going through the jobs section of the *Evening Standard* with a biro, ringing round anything that looked vaguely promising. Words stared up at her like indifferent strangers. *Excellent interpersonal skills. In-depth knowledge of Excel. A challenging and varied role, in which you'll* . . . Her heart briefly leapt at the sight of the word *Admin*, then plummeted again as she took in the rest. *Superb opportunity for an experienced head of admin to join this prestigious advertising agency in Soho.* Nothing for her there. Far too senior. She sighed, and moved her hand to the edge of the paper, prepared to turn the page.

Suddenly something pulled her eyes back to the job she'd just looked at. She read it properly for the first time. Strange, but she'd always thought of admin in terms of shops, supermarkets, council offices. In terms of Underlyme. She'd never associated it with advertising agencies, simply because there hadn't *been* any, back home.

It was like a tingle in her mind, a pins-and-needles feeling rapidly giving way to the butterflies of true excitement. *If I was you, I'd keep an eye out for another admin job,* the young woman in the recruitment agency had said, and Rachel had smiled across the table and said, *They're taking on new people all over the place.*

There's an admin department where Rachel works. There's got to be . . .

Cotton-mouthed, she rose from her chair, headed for the wardrobe and her denim jacket. Reaching into the pocket for her wallet, she opened it with hands that shook slightly. The business card was there, tucked in with her Underlyme library card. *Rachel Carter, Account Manager,* she read, then, skimming down, *Central Switchboard* . . .

Far too late to call now. She'd ring tomorrow, ask to be put through to the admin department, ask if they were still looking for people. It was as if she'd been trudging through an endless desert and suddenly saw buildings at last, tiny on the horizon, but there.

She thought she'd have trouble sleeping, with the prospect of phone calls and interviews chasing round and round her mind. But she didn't.

She did, however, have a very strange dream.

18

She woke up in her room in Camden. Through the window she saw the bright afternoon sunlight, the willow tree and shed that belonged in Underlyme. It was the garden from Acacia Avenue, she saw with delight. It seemed perfectly natural that it should be here, it always *had* been there, always *would* be.

Jumping out of bed, she bounded down the stairs, seeing without surprise that she'd become twelve again – she could remember the pink Snoopy pyjamas, the longer, blonder hair that tumbled round her face. With wild and childish joy she raced out into melting summer, feeling the sun hot on her face and the grass warm beneath her feet, seeing the well-tended flowerbeds as bright splashes of colour on the lawn.

Catching a glimpse of something white on one of the roses, she went over, vaguely curious. It was pinned to a thorn as if to a notice board, and she picked it off carefully. It was an elegant little business card. *Rachel Carter*, it said, *Account Manager*. She was looking at it closely, wondering how this not-quite-remembered item could have strayed in – had it been blown, perhaps? Had a bird brought it here? – when the black writing suddenly disappeared in a blob of dissolving indigo. She looked up, and although the light was still summery and beautiful, the sky was apocalyptic, laden with charcoal-coloured storm clouds, pelting, pounding rain.

And worse. This was chemical rain, she realised, acid rain, radioactive. Wherever it touched, she could see the bright primary colours draining away to something strange and muted. A red rose faded to yellowish-brown as she watched, the bushes seemed in the middle of some terrible wilting decay. And as she glanced down at the card still clenched in her hand, her slow, hypnotised dismay turned into horror, because her own skin was draining of colour along with the card in her hand.

She started to run towards the open back door and it seemed further away than it ever had, the length of a football pitch. Her father stood in the doorway, familiar and reassuring. She was about to run past him, expecting him to usher her into safety, but he moved to block her out, hands barring her on both sides, dissolving as the flowers did, as the world did. He opened his mouth, and spoke in Rachel's voice.

You're lying, he said, and as she felt herself beginning to fade, she attempted desperately to push past him. Again he blocked her, then his hand came down on her shoulder. His touch brought a new and swooning terror, because the pressure of his fingers was too intimate, somehow, too *knowing*, and her dream-skin rose into hard lumps of gooseflesh in the same split second as she woke up.

Book Two

This afternoon, I decided what I'm going to do. It's not like I've got any choice.

They're off the day after tomorrow. I heard them talking about packing earlier, and it made my mind up. Because he was there too, in the kitchen with the rest of us. While they were talking, he kept looking at me. It was the same kind of look she used to give me, before all this started, when we were stuck listening to the grown-ups boring each other to death, when we were best friends. A look that sort of said we've got a secret.

I always thought it was just something people said, it makes my flesh crawl. But when I saw him looking at me, that's how it felt. Like my skin was crawling with something, beetles and spiders walking all over it.

She's got to believe me. That's what I decided in the kitchen. I'm going to get her alone tomorrow, in the garden. And I'm going to tell her everything.

She'll never go away and leave me alone with him when she knows what's going to happen when it's just me here. She'll pretend she's ill or something and stay – she'd have to be evil to walk away after I'd told her everything. She'd have to be the worst person in the world.

She's going to listen. And she's going to stay.

Tomorrow, she's going to know—

1

It was the last Friday in May, and Rachel was sitting in her new office going over some client notes for a meeting the following morning when she heard the knock at the door. She turned her eyes and mind from the computer screen. 'Come in.'

Diane opened the door. 'Good news, Rach,' she announced breezily. 'Not too busy to hear it, are you?'

'Of course not. Come on in.'

The familiar sounds of the open-plan main office were abruptly cut off as Diane closed the door and sat down in a world of senior-level silence. Rachel watched her holding unspecified good news behind her back like an arch adult with a treat for a favoured child. Carefully she concealed her own impatience. 'So, what is it?' she asked, with a deliberate smile. 'Not being promoted again, am I?'

The Queen Vic laugh, sounding loud enough to filter through the closed office door. 'Sorry, Rach, even you're not ready for my job *just* yet. But it's almost as good. We've been invited to pitch for the Fiat account.'

'Well, that's good news. Worth a lot of money, isn't it?'

'Just a bit.' Rachel struggled to hide her slight confusion as Diane nodded, her eyes glinting like water. 'And it's not just good news for the agency, Rach. It's good news for *you*. I want you to lead it.'

A long silence; no sound from beyond the double-glazed window, through the thick office door. 'God,' said Rachel slowly, at last. 'Do you think I'm ready?'

In her shock, she'd spoken without thinking. She had her first ever glimpse of the Diane so feared and hated in office gossip, the cold metallic edge like the flash of a knife. 'If I didn't think so, Rachel, I wouldn't have fought like I did to get you promoted. You better believe *that.*' Then the laugh came, and Rachel was facing the Diane she knew again; a bit bawdy, a bit girly, the ideal East End aunt. 'You can handle it, Rach. I thought you liked a challenge?'

'Well, of course. You know that.' Another moment's silence. Rachel spoke again with bright, assumed fearlessness, aware that any sign of uncertainty could make that knife flash again. Very much not wanting to see it a second time. 'So when do we start winning it?'

'*That's* more like it.' Diane's smile was as dazzling as the peacock-blue of her skirt suit. 'There's going to be a first-stage meeting next Monday morning, in the boardroom. I'll be there to hold your hand for that. But when the real work starts, Rach, you're going to be the one behind the wheel. *You'll* get the team together, *you'll* brief the creatives, and *you'll* kick their arse if they don't deliver top-notch stuff. And, I almost forgot. You're going to present back to the client, on the big day.'

'God,' said Rachel again, then remembered how suddenly that face and voice could change. 'It's just what I wanted, Diane. I can't believe it.'

'I knew it wouldn't faze you, Rach. Senior account handlers can't afford to get scared about responsibility.' The deafening laughter rang out. 'Well, put it in your diary, then,' she said. 'Boardroom, nine sharp, Monday. Don't be late.' Then the office door was closing, leaving Rachel alone and in silence.

Jesus Christ, she thought dimly. A part of her had known, must have known, what this promotion would involve, but she found the reality suddenly unsettling. She'd played an important part behind the scenes of the Fanta pitch, but compared to this, it looked like work experience paper-shuffling. The difference between a driving lesson and taking to the roads in a foreign country, alone . . .

On an impulse, she dialled Andrew's work number. 'I don't believe it. I just found out I'm going to be leading a major pitch.'

'It just keeps getting better for you, doesn't it? Congratulations again – you must be celebrating!'

It was obvious he'd misread the quiet tension in her voice, interpreted it as the kind that could snap into euphoria at any second, and she was about to set him straight when she imagined his doubt and surprise. It would only drive home her essential difference from the all-conquering public façade; the woman he'd fallen in love with. 'Not quite yet,' she said, and heard confidence flooding back into her words as she spoke. 'But I'm happy. I've been waiting for something like this for *years.*'

'You deserve it. Well done.' And then the phone went down in Rachel's ear.

2

Andrew sat at his desk, trying to read a work e-mail, while his mind was running on a different track completely. The only word he could think of was *Rachel.*

He remembered the conversation they'd had in the Fulham flat a couple of weeks ago. Him and Rachel and Helen, gathered round the kitchen table. *I like novelty,* he'd said, *but I like an easy life more.* He hadn't realised it at the time, but he was starting to think it was one of the most telling statements he'd ever made. It was why he'd fallen in love with Rachel, and why he was starting to have serious doubts about their whole relationship.

They'd been together just over a year now. Before they'd met, all the girls he'd known had been much like his sister and her friends: bounding, ebullient young women, cheerful and uncomplicated as Labrador puppies. Pleasant company, in their undemanding way, but far too familiar to be fascinating. At first-date stage, he could guess at every detail of their lives, the kind of house they'd grown up in, the kind of friends they hung out with, the kind of job they had. And later dates would always prove him right. A constant sense of something missing, some element of challenge, of mystery. There was nothing to discover in them; their lives were open books.

But Rachel ... from the start of their relationship, he'd known she was different. She was more serious and more intelligent and more focused, but there was far more to it than that. He never quite knew what she was thinking, and the occasional glimpses he got of her real self intrigued him. Nina Carter hadn't been at all what he'd expected – he'd been prepared for a high-powered overachiever, and amiable, hippyish Nina had taken him completely by surprise. Then there was Rachel's apparent lack of other ties, the assorted detritus of old schoolmates and old uni mates and group events that he'd always taken for granted as an integral part of life. At some level she seemed detached from the only world he knew, and before they'd moved in together, that had been an endless source of fascination; ultimately exotic and mysterious, a woman who travelled alone.

Over the last month, however, all that had changed. Now, what had attracted him most was becoming very off-putting. He looked at his live-in girlfriend, and saw a stranger looking back.

He didn't like to acknowledge to himself what had first alerted him, made him see her in a different light. But he knew perfectly well: it was sex. Before they'd moved in together, they'd seen each other perhaps twice a week, due to the demands of their respective jobs, and the physical side of their relationship had been necessarily occasional. So he'd found it easy to overlook how different she could be at those times. It stood to reason: sometimes you just weren't in the mood, other times you were.

Now they were living together, however, he'd come to realise that it was nowhere near that simple. Sometimes she took him aback with her wildness – it wasn't the kind you'd expect from a girlfriend, there was no sense of affection, of joy in physical contact. There was something feverish and compulsive about it; a kind of desperation in her clutching hands, her sharp cries that sounded far more like pain than pleasure. As if she was forcing herself to do something she loathed. And at other times, she was as stiff and unresponsive as a plank of wood, enduring in silence, eyes tight shut as if to block him out. She was the only woman he'd ever met who insisted on having the light on during sex, but he increasingly longed to turn it off; the sight of her urgency was as unnerving as the sight of her coldness.

His realisation of her sexual schizophrenia had changed everything, made him see her in a different way. Her near-obsessive cleanness and tidiness, the way she didn't even drink on special occasions. The way she had colleagues, instead of friends, people she occasionally met up with for lunch. Nobody she spoke to on a regular basis at all, apart from that incongruous mother. While she wasn't part of his sister's inner circle, he sometimes thought Helen was the closest thing to a real female friend she had. Instead of exciting rootlessness, he'd come to sense a bone-deep isolation, unfathomable, alien, troubling.

Their relationship had begun to disturb him, he realised. It was like living with a pleasant stranger, except it wasn't at all. You couldn't think of someone as *pleasant* when you had no idea what they were hiding behind their back; what secrets their charming smile concealed as they did so. *Pleasant* demanded a sense of trust...

But he didn't want to think about that. It implied too clearly what he didn't want to face – the fact that he might have made a serious mistake by moving in with her. The phone rang on his desk, jolting him back to the immediacy of the office, and he plunged into it again with a deep sense of relief.

3

Sophie followed the directions she'd been given out of Farringdon station. As she turned a corner, she fixed her eyes and thoughts on the BHN building. She saw it with infinite longing, like something glittering behind an exclusive shop window in the Christmas season. Pale sunlight glinted and sparkled off the windows.

Inside, the cold breeze was replaced by the deliberate chill of air-conditioning. The vastness of the building struck her out of nowhere. She found it easy to imagine the new Rachel Carter walking through here like an actress from a shampoo ad, artfully careless dark bob swinging. She wanted to belong here herself.

On the first floor, an archway led on to a scene of casual activity. She imagined herself on the phone to Julie or Lisa or Marianne, describing *my office, my workmates, my desk.* 'Excuse me,' she said, approaching the nearest desk, 'I've got an interview with Lisa Shah, at twelve noon. I'm a bit early, I'm afraid.'

'Don't worry about it. I'll go and let her know you're here.'

The girl at the desk walked away, and Sophie stood stock-still, steady office noise washing over her from all sides. Four days ago, she'd had a lengthy interview with the woman named Lisa Shah over the phone, had tentatively hoped this face-to-face encounter was nothing more than a formality. She wished she could believe that now . . .

'Sophie? Hi, I'm Lisa.'

The twenty-something Indian woman walking towards her fitted in here, but nowhere near as intimidatingly as Sophie had feared. She didn't look so different from women she'd known in Underlyme. 'Hi,' she said, 'nice to meet you,' and she extended a hand for shaking, feeling her nervousness diminish even as her longing intensified.

In a pleasant little side office with colourful charts on the walls, an infinity of tiny stars zoomed on a screen-saver. Lisa got down to business straightaway. 'Well, as I told you last Friday, we've never been busier here,' she said. 'To be honest, it's pretty hectic.'

'It's all right,' Sophie said quickly. 'I'm used to hard work.'

'Good. Well, you wouldn't be doing anything you're not used to. Filing and record-keeping, mostly, and faxing, answering the phone, all the usual.' Sophie nodded earnestly, tentatively. 'If you joined us, you'd be on probation for the first month. After that, if you wanted to, you might be able to branch out. Would that appeal to you?'

Sophie had no idea whether it was good or bad to say yes. A compromise came out on its own. 'I think so.'

'Well, we've got good promotion opportunities here, if you're interested. But let's not get ahead of ourselves.' The last sentence sent Sophie's hopes plummeting – she'd been overconfident, she wasn't going to get it – but then Lisa spoke again. 'I'd be very pleased for you to join us here, Sophie. And I think you'd like it too.'

She went on to discuss holiday, salary and benefits. They were all unexceptional, but, sitting across the desk, Sophie couldn't have cared less. She felt her surroundings undergo some small but crucial change; the difference between a longed-for item and one finally possessed, less mysterious, more detailed, tangible.

When she finally left the building, she discovered truth in a cliché as she found herself walking on air, and the colours around her seemed brighter and more vivid than they'd ever done before. Only five days to go, she thought, till she'd be coming here again. She went into the underground, and headed back to Camden.

4

When Rachel got in from work, Andrew wasn't home. She was pouring herself a glass of orange juice when the phone rang in the hallway, and she turned from the kitchen to get it.

'Hi, Rachel. It's me,' said Nina. 'Haven't called at a bad time, have I?'

Rachel realised she must have sounded slightly breathless and distracted. 'Not at all, I'm fine,' she said quickly. 'Just got back from the office.'

'How's it going, now you've been promoted?'

More than anything, Rachel wanted to express her subtle new anxiety, the look in Diane's eyes. But something held the words back, and she heard her own carefree voice. 'Oh, very well. Much the same.'

'That's great. You'll never guess who I heard from today.'

'Who?'

'Linda. She just rang up out of the blue,' Nina carried on cheerfully. 'She sounds different, now she's remarried. More relaxed.'

Rachel struggled to speak normally. 'What did she want?'

'Oh, nothing much. Just to get back in touch properly. I think she's trying to make a new start, to be honest. She's right, it's silly we're so distant when we only live half an hour's drive apart. It's no secret I couldn't get on with that Brian, but now . . .'

'Did she mention Sophie?'

'Only to say she's moved to Camden as well. Funny you're both in the same place now. Who knows, you might even run into her.' A moment in which Rachel might have interrupted, then Nina carried on. 'It seemed like Linda didn't know that much about it. Incredible, when it's her only child. I must say, it doesn't sound like they're at all close these days.'

Seconds of silence, laden with undercurrents that only Rachel knew, and Nina's total unawareness. 'It would be nice if you could meet up again, you two. You used to be best friends, after all, before you had that silly fight – and that's all in the past now.'

'Well,' said Rachel evasively, 'maybe.'

'I could get you her number from Linda. She's sure to have that.'

'Oh, no.' Rachel had a sense of some crucial boundary being violated; she spoke hastily. 'I don't think it's such a good idea. We haven't spoken in so long, it would feel strange. There's no point getting back in touch.'

'Well. If you're sure. I'd better get on – the cat needs feeding. Have a good evening.'

'You too. Speak to you soon.'

Off the phone, Rachel told herself it was nothing, there wasn't anything to worry about. There was still a safe distance between Sophie and herself, the distance she'd relied on in some way for over ten years. Her anxiety about the pitch was simply spreading into areas it had nothing to do with. Walking back into the kitchen, she made a start on dinner, and waited for Andrew to come home.

5

Saturday afternoon in Camden. The very beginning of June and feeling like it. Wandering aimlessly through the market, Sophie felt her lack of immediate purpose like a holiday, a lull before her imminent start at BHN. It seemed that relaxation was something like a long lie-in; you could only enjoy it when you had something to contrast it with, the certain prospect of activity in the future.

She moved through the deafening crowds, beginning to enjoy this new freedom. The seeds of a real life here had been planted. She was young and single in the capital, and more alive than she could remember feeling in years.

Fourteen years, maybe? something whispered in her mind. As if to turn away from it, she changed direction, towards the open-air café in the market itself, where she sat with a Diet Coke and a jacket potato. Nearby, a small child swung off the back of a chair as off a climbing frame, and an irritable maternal voice rose above the clamour. 'Don't do that, Daisy,' it was yelling, 'you'll break your ankle.' Sophie wondered if she'd see Rachel when she started at BHN. She didn't think so. It seemed too big for the two of them to run into each other.

She'd phoned her mother yesterday, to tell her about the new job. A perfunctory call, amiable, but oddly impersonal; over in a matter of minutes, laden with the kind of phrases nodding acquaintances used to each other in lifts and bus queues. *Well, that's nice. Good luck. I'm sure you'll be very happy there.* Not a conversation between a mother and an only child at all, especially not an only child who'd lived at home for twenty-five years. Yet Sophie's continued stay in Acacia Avenue had felt as impersonal as the shared house in Camden: you tidied up after yourself, you smiled and nodded and made small talk when your paths crossed, you touched each other's lives not at all.

Incredible, to think they used to be so close. The Perfect Suburban Mother and the Perfect Suburban Daughter, a dream team. Mrs Townsend dropping little Sophie off at school, taking her shopping in Poole and Bournemouth on Saturdays, chaperoning birthday trips to ice rinks and cinemas, presiding over the celebrations afterwards. Marks and Spencer's birthday cakes and party games in the lounge. Not elaborate like the parties of a couple of girls in her year, who'd lived in the wealthy Preston suburbs and had bouncy castles and kids' entertainers and goodie bags containing things you actually kept, but *solid* parties, *unjudgeable* parties. Like everything else about her life, safely in the top ten per cent . . .

Her father was never around at those times. He was usually working. He was a tall, lanky man with a long, bean-shaped face, flaring nostrils, small colourless eyes – starting to go bald, carrying with him a faint, unplaceable smell like horseradish.

His braying voice showcased a pedantic way of talking, unusually elaborate sentence structures that seemed to require brackets and semi-colons. He was a police inspector, and kept strange hours.

But he and her mother always came to the big events. School nativity plays, sports days, parents' evenings, where the teachers gave good reports of hard work and popularity and all the other benchmarks of primary-school attainment. St William's Primary School, she remembered, the happiest days of her life . . .

What it had been like at this time of year, in the summer term. Short essays and pictures mounted on coloured card, gold colouring pens and the class computer, and God, how it all came flooding back – it felt like a hose turning on in her mind, a high-pressure jet of memory. Skipping games, and pencil tins, and plimsolls, and—

walking with Rachel across the playground, on the second-to-last day of the summer term. The distant roar of Junior Four boys playing football on the field. The thin, shrill shriek of a dinner lady's whistle. Their own delighted voices.

'*Mum says it's fine, Rach! You can stay for the whole summer!*'

'*Daisy!* If you don't stop doing that, you're going to get a smacked bum!'

The furious maternal voice from the next table jerked Sophie abruptly from her reverie. That remembered playground had been so real in her mind, it was like waking up from a vivid dream. Strange, she thought, how it had all looked so safe and peaceful and beguiling. At the time, she'd had no idea what was going to follow.

She finished her food, got up from the table and wandered back towards the shared house. Its impersonality no longer worried her. She had something else now, a kind of home in her mind; a place where she'd be expected on Monday morning.

6

'So that's settled,' said Rachel, 'July the twenty-fifth it is.'

Eleven thirty, and she was sitting in her office with Sara and Christina, who'd been put on the Fiat pitch with her. They'd just got back from Fiat's London head office, where they'd taken the brief. 'Don't worry,' said Christina, and Sara nodded, and they smiled variations on a neat, flirty little mutual smile – Christina's girlish, Sara's more predatory. 'We'll put it in our diaries.'

'Good to hear it. We've got a month and a half on this, and that's plenty of time. But only if we use it right. First off, we'll have to get a team on it. I'm hoping for Craig and Neil.'

Nods across the desk. Craig and Neil were the agency's acknowledged creative superstars, hot from a string of recent awards. 'I'll call the creative director,' Rachel continued, 'and check they're free to work on it. If so, I'd like to brief them in ASAP.'

'What if they're not free to take the brief right away?' asked Christina.

'Then we wait till they are. So long as it happens in the next week.' Nods again, then silence. Rachel checked her watch deliberately. 'That should be all,' she said. 'For now.'

Brief words of assent and goodbye, then Sara and Christina left. Alone at her desk, Rachel waited till the door had shut behind them before releasing a long, pressurised breath. Nothing had gone wrong that morning exactly – they had a detailed brief, clear guidelines to work with – but, far from going away, her worries were deepening. There was so much here that she'd never done before, and the thought scared her. One false step, and there'd be nobody to block the fall—

Don't be ridiculous. You're not going to fall – why should you? Still, the possibility existed, and carried fear along with it like a shadow. It was all up to her now. Diane had made her responsible, but she liked Sara and Christina little, and trusted them less. For the first time, she had the terrible suspicion that she'd been promoted far beyond her experience and abilities; that the people who'd questioned her advancement might have had an extremely good point.

You'll manage, she reassured herself, and the voice became her mother's voice, long ago, in Underlyme. *You're so efficient, Rachel. So responsible. I wouldn't be surprised if you were Prime Minister when you grow up—*

A knock at the door. 'Come in.'

It was Peter. As always, she felt the tension in the air before the mundanity came, the inevitable and the expected. 'Hi, Peter,' she said. 'How are you?'

'Not bad. I see you're going up in the world.'

If his words admired the office, his tone did anything but, implying a deep, detached, cynical indifference to all it meant. Again, Rachel grabbed at a cliché. 'Can't complain.'

Their eyes met for a second too long before he spoke again. 'So – want anything from Pret?'

'I'll have the Miracle Mayo Thai Chicken, please.'

He wrote on his pad. Another second of electric silence, a moment trembling on the edge of the unknown. It reached the furthest point of balance, then righted itself.

'Okay,' he said, and left.

Rachel sat and looked out through the glass partition that blocked her off from the open-plan office. Watching him walking away, she felt what she always felt at these times – a dark fascination approaching intrigue, something furtive and creeping that could never quite acknowledge its own existence.

7

She couldn't understand how the people around her didn't seem to notice Peter at all. Watching through the glass, she saw their indifference all over again – casual glances that looked without seeing a thing. The clothes he wore seemed like some curiously impenetrable comic-book disguise, jeans and trainers effective as Clark Kent's suit. Adding up to a typical young man from a nondescript background: low IQ, few GCSEs, banal concerns revolving round motorbikes and one-night stands, shabby night-spots, a mumbling gaggle of identikit mates.

Incredible, how unobservant people were. As far as Kate was concerned, Rachel thought, it wasn't that surprising – cheerfully slapdash Kate, so obviously bored by subtle nuances. But Sara and Christina also ignored him, and their sharp little eyes were exquisitely attuned to detail, sweeping over people like supermarket scanners, alert to a metal filling, a fake Ralph Lauren shirt. It seemed to Rachel that the quality that fascinated her was too subtle to register on their state-of-the-art equipment – you couldn't plot it on a radar screen any more than you could plot an emotion.

But every time Rachel looked at Peter, she was profoundly aware of his strangeness. The veneer of dull normality was transparent to her eyes, revealing a surprisingly long list of *exceptionallys* – exceptionally thin, exceptionally pale. His eyes were exceptionally large and blue, his face exceptionally expressionless. He looked like a drawing by a talented artist with no essential interest in people, who set eyes, nose and mouth together as they'd have set the component parts of a car. Everything was in the right place, but something jarred slightly – some crucial sense of life not there.

His expression only changed when he talked to her, and then only very slightly. He would have been self-possessed for thirty, although he couldn't have been more than eighteen; even in her presence, he was quiet, serious, detached. But every time they spoke, Rachel could see her own fascination reflecting back, saw a part of herself too clearly in his eyes. He reminded her too deeply of her old self, and while she didn't like to recognise that, it couldn't be denied – a lost and restless thing that moved in darkness, and belonged nowhere . . .

He was leaving the office now. She watched him disappear

from sight, then yanked her eyes back to the photograph on her desk, denying the extent of an interest that haunted her intermittently. There was nothing of her in that strange and silent loneliness, the indifference to the world that defined true isolation. She belonged to bright and open places now, this office, and the flat in Camden, and the light—

She thought of the bottles in the garage shop, the house in Acacia Avenue, and brushed the images away a split second before they could settle.

Andrew smiled from the frame with his arm round her shoulder. An e-mail appeared in the bottom right-hand side of her computer screen. The air-con murmured soothingly and the world was as it should be, and she forced Peter from her thoughts before phoning the creative director about Craig and Neil.

8

'Want to get some lunch, Soph?'

The girl called Jessie Mott looked about seventeen, bright, blonde and perky. Sophie had taken to her at once. As she approached Sophie's desk, Sophie looked up and smiled. 'I'd love to.'

Out of the office, waiting for a lift, Jessie turned to her. 'So how you liking it so far?'

'It's hard to tell, really. It's only my second day.' The lift arrived, and they stepped in. 'How long have you been working here?'

'Too long,' said Jessie, and laughed. 'About a year now. Joined right after GCSEs – seems like I've been here all my life.'

'What do you think of it?'

'Oh, it's all right. Lisa's a bit strict, but she's a good laugh sometimes. The rest of the admin lot all talk about their kids too much, but they're mostly harmless.' A sharp electric *ping!* – they stepped out into reception. 'To be honest, I'm really glad you've joined. It's nice to have someone my own age here at last.'

Sophie smiled. 'You might be disappointed. I'm twenty-five.'

'You're joking. You look about eighteen – if that.' They strolled out into the afternoon. 'Well, I'm still glad you've joined. So long as you promise not to talk about knitting patterns.'

'Or my grandchildren,' said Sophie gravely. 'I promise.'

They walked on a little further in amiable silence, before Jessie spoke again. 'You know, you really joined at the right time. It's the Royal Academy do in a couple of weeks.'

'What's that?'

'Haven't you heard?' Jessie glanced at her in surprise. 'Big company event at that art gallery in Piccadilly. There's champagne and food, and it doesn't finish till really late. I went last year, and it was great.' She broke off for a second, grimaced. 'Mind you, we'll get stuck with reception duty again. That's a pain in the neck.'

'What's reception duty?'

'When clients turn up, we have to say hi and all that,' Jessie said glumly. 'Mind you, nobody has to do more than fifteen minutes. We'll get the rota sent round on the e-mail nearer the time. There's something for you to look forward to.'

Sophie suddenly thought of Rachel. 'Do the account managers have to do it with us?' she asked, trying to sound casual.

'Not the senior ones. Supposed to be too busy *liaising with clients* – getting hammered and having a chat, in other words.' Intense relief washed over Sophie. Jessie grinned. 'But our lot always do. Worse luck.'

'I don't mind,' said Sophie, and then they were going into a crowded little sandwich shop, joining the considerable queue, where chat subsided. Jessie was served first, and waited by the drinks counter for Sophie to join her. 'That's the best place to go for lunch round here,' she confided as they walked back out into the sunlight. 'There's a Pret up the road, but the prices are scary. You know, they get Pret food for free on the account handlers' floor.'

'Yeah?'

'For real, every lunchtime. My brother brings them round, does odd jobs round the building as well. It's a full-time job. It was me who told him about it. He hadn't worked for a while, and I knew he could do with the money.'

'It must be good,' said Sophie. 'Having him in the same building.'

'Well – maybe.' Jessie's shrug was awkward and embarrassed. 'We've never exactly been close. I worry about him sometimes.'

Sophie didn't want to pry, but couldn't hide her sudden interest. 'What's wrong with him?'

'Oh, I don't know. He's a strange one, Peter.'

They approached the BHN building in silence, Sophie wanting to know more, prevented from asking by Jessie's apparent unease with the subject.

Back in the office, however, curiosity faded quickly. It was immensely busy, insanely busy, and five thirty seemed to arrive out of nowhere. Out of the corner of her eye, she saw Jessie approaching her desk. 'You coming, Soph? I'll hold the lift for you.'

'No, really, it's okay. I want to finish this off before I go home.' She did; she'd been given no deadline for the filing that currently occupied her, but knew she'd feel bad about leaving it for the morning. 'See you tomorrow.'

'Well, see you tomorrow. Don't work too hard.' Jessie left.

By six thirty, the office was virtually empty, and the filing almost complete. Lisa Shah came out of her private side office, did a double-take as she saw Sophie. 'Still hard at work?' she asked, then, approaching Sophie's desk and buttoning her jacket up, 'You don't have to stay this late. It'll wait till the morning.'

'Oh, really, I might as well get it finished. There's hardly anything left to do.' Sophie felt slightly awkward; smiled her apologetic, embarrassed determination across the desk. 'I won't be more than fifteen minutes.'

'Such dedication. I'm quite impressed.' The smile that reflected back at her was neat, distant, approving. 'Well, if you're sure. Have a nice evening.'

Sophie finished ten minutes later. Relieved to have completed it at last, she checked her watch and saw it was almost seven o'clock. It didn't matter, she thought, there was no hurry to get back to the house.

By the lifts, she pressed the button and waited – tired, contented, unselfconscious. Then a lift arrived, and as the doors slid open, her mood snapped instantly into something else. Two women stood inside it: one a big-boned redhead with messy corkscrew curls; the other Rachel.

9

The world froze for a moment. Deep down, Sophie hadn't expected to encounter Rachel in this building at all, never mind here and now. Their eyes met, with a too-strong echo of Underlyme town centre, an October afternoon. Sophie stepped in.

'Hi, Rachel,' she said, as the lift doors closed behind her.

'Sophie?' Still they stared at each other in the harsh white light, as the floor fell away beneath their feet. 'What are you doing here?'

'I'm working here now.' Inexplicably, it sounded like an admission, a confession. 'I started yesterday.'

The doors opened and all three of them stepped out. Sophie saw the big redhead hovering, nakedly curious, as they stopped directly outside the lifts. Part of her expected an introduction, but Rachel made none. 'Bye, Kate,' she said absently, 'see you.' There was nothing Kate could do but walk away with a backward glance. Despite herself, Sophie was startled by the curt efficiency of that dismissal, before she looked at Rachel more closely, saw the extent of Rachel's preoccupation.

'Well.' It was as if Rachel didn't quite know what to say – spoke words scripted but not learned by heart, a bad actress reading off paper. 'What a coincidence.'

'Not really,' said Sophie awkwardly. 'I got the idea from you. When you said they were looking for people here . . .'

Silence fell, and it occurred to her how she'd imagined Rachel looking in this reception. It was true, she did look like an actress in the right stage-set, a shock revelation in the last seconds of a glossy soap. Everything around them had the look of scenery. 'I didn't mention your name,' she went on, suddenly defensive. 'Just rang up, the week before last. Had an interview on the phone.'

Another lift across from them stopped; the sharp metallic *ding!* as a couple of middle-aged men in suits walked out. 'You see, the target figure's going down all the time,' one was saying earnestly. 'It would be ridiculous to think . . .' Then they were out of earshot, approaching the revolving doors. Rachel didn't seem to have noticed them.

'You must have got the number from my business card,' she said at last.

'That's right.' Again, the tone was straight from a confessional. She had an overwhelming urge to mitigate, to obscurely reassure. 'It's just in the admin department. Nothing much, really.'

'Enjoying it so far?'

Rachel read the words laboriously from the unseen script while Sophie looked for her own next line over Rachel's shoulder, eyes flicking to the evening beyond reception. 'Well, yeah. I suppose so.'

'Good.' She had a sense of Rachel pulling herself together with an effort; the uncertain voice became brisk and casually professional. 'Which way are you walking?'

'I'm not. I'm meeting someone in here, in a few minutes.' Suddenly, Sophie feared being caught up in an interminable walk to the tube station, this conversation dragging on; this inexplicable feeling of guilt, a clearly understood inference that she had no business here. 'Just a friend,' she continued, as the silence pressed in. 'She doesn't work here.'

'I'll be off, then. Have a good evening.' Rachel's smile was bright, charming and unconvincing. 'Expect I'll see you round.'

'Bye, Rach.'

Sophie stood and watched her walk away – heard the three-inch heels ringing out sharp and hollow on the faux-marble, saw the revolving door turn a retreating back into darkness. She waited another five minutes before leaving herself, just out of sight of the reception desk, leaning back on the cold, smooth wall. Something in Rachel's eyes, behind the bad-actress curiosity, irresistibly reminding Sophie of—

Acacia Avenue, fourteen years ago. The sense of something dangerous lying in wait, preparing to spring. The horror of those words behind the garden shed – the words of hysterical rejection that had haunted her ever since—

You're lying!

But that was ridiculous. Time must have blunted those words, made them harmless at last. They'd both changed beyond recognition from the little girls they'd been then. Sophie took a long, deep breath and started walking, through reception, into the evening.

10

Andrew wasn't back when Rachel let herself in. She locked the door behind her, saw her hands were trembling slightly. *The cold*, she told herself. *It's a chilly night for June.* But the sight of Sophie Townsend in reception had shaken her badly. That face and voice, so infinitely redolent of the past, thrown randomly into her present life.

She put all the lights on, poured herself a glass of pineapple juice in the kitchen. In the living room, she switched the TV on, but she couldn't concentrate. Remembering what Nina had said over the phone, she felt both terrified and defensive, as if her life was in some way being broken into. To think that Sophie was now working at BHN. The only person in the world who knew all her secrets . . .

Strange, to remember how it had once been between them. Thinking back to St William's Primary School, Rachel found memories of her life there preserved like bugs in amber: the junior debating team, the chess club, the library rota. Gold stars on the schoolwork and straight As on the annual report card. Nina's bewildered pride, that seemed to admire her daughter more the less that daughter resembled her.

I don't know where she gets it from, Rachel heard her saying to a boyfriend. *I was never anywhere near that brainy, and I know for a fact her dad wasn't.*

The long-vanished father she'd never known. Cheerfully irresponsible Nina, who felt more like a chatty big sister than a mum. Nina's interests largely revolved around men, and mates, and brief fads that she lost interest in weeks after discovering them – yoga, Buddhism, meditation. She made no secret of the fact that she worked purely to live, a succession of temporary jobs she had no real interest in. Rachel implied an entirely different family background, conventional, success-driven parents stamped through and through with the Protestant work ethic – a reserved, hardworking, earnest sort of child, a conscientious worrier. She had friends in her year, but no real intimates. In some way, she always felt much older than she was, more interested in school marks than birthday parties, in reading books than gossip.

Maybe it was because she and Sophie were so different that they'd become best friends. Vivacious, giggly little Sophie Townsend, crown princess of the My Little Pony fan club. The teachers liked her as much as her peers did, but she was nobody's hot tip for head girl. Even though Rachel was a year older, they'd quickly become inseparable, a permanent fixture in the playground at breaktimes and lunch hours, spending evenings and weekends at one another's homes.

The cramped, cheerful little flat near Underlyme's town centre. The big, prosperous, conventional family home on Acacia Avenue . . .

Rachel jerked out of her reverie abruptly, afraid of surrender to the past. No point remembering all that now. Andrew had cooked last night, she'd better get the dinner on. Out in the kitchen, she washed, dried and replaced the glass she'd been drinking from, drew the blinds against the night. Images of Sophie drifted through a closed-off part of her mind, with images of the Fiat pitch, and Peter.

11

When she came into the office next morning, Kate was already at her desk. 'Morning,' said Rachel, pausing on the way to her own office. 'In early, aren't you?'

'Got some stuff to catch up on. Should have stayed later last night, really,' said Kate. 'By the way, who's that girl you were talking to in the lift?'

'Oh, someone I know. She's just started here.' Rachel hurried to change the subject before further questions could be asked. 'Looking forward to the Royal Academy?'

'Oh, yeah. But I just know I'm going to be stuck on reception again. It's all right for you, you'll never get roped in now you've been promoted.' A couple more people came into the office. 'Suppose you're bringing Andrew?'

'Sure am. Not that I'll see much of him – I'll be stuck with clients all night,' said Rachel. 'Anyway, better get to work. See you later.'

The morning passed slowly. At half eleven, Sara and Christina came into her office for a catch-up. Rachel drew the blinds at the glass wall panels to say *do not disturb*. The blinds at the windows were open, showing a perfect morning from three floors up. 'I called the creative director yesterday,' Rachel said, sitting down at her desk. 'Craig and Neil can work on it, but they won't be free to take the brief till next Friday.'

'Maybe we should get another team assigned,' said Sara.

'I don't think so. Next Friday's less than ten days away – it won't make any difference.' She saw dubious eyes fixed on her. The sight unsettled her, and she carried on almost curtly. 'I want Craig and Neil on this pitch. They're far and away the best team for this kind of thing, and I'm very pleased they're free.'

'But it's still going to hold us up,' said Christina.

'It doesn't have to. There's plenty we can be getting on with.' She heard her voice like a stranger's; chilly, decisive. 'We need to get everything arranged with the research department. And the media costings – they're going to be very important.'

Various minor tasks were assigned, then Sara and Christina left, thinly veiled doubt strong on the air. When the door had closed behind them, Rachel felt deeply uncertain. She could see time slipping away if they waited for Craig and Neil, but at the same time, she could hear a dismissive voice down a receiver: *to be honest, none of us thought the work was quite creative enough, we're looking for an agency that's going to win us awards.* It was like a tug-of-war in her head – she'd stayed with her original decision more out of desperation than anything else. Had to come down on one side or the other, sound as if she meant it.

More than ever, she realised the terrifying weight of responsibility. The way her thoughts stuttered and tangled up in themselves drove it home to her as nothing else could. Thinking *who can I ask*, and realising there was nobody; thinking *maybe I'll go to Diane*, and realising that she couldn't. Like a tiring swimmer, she put her feet down casually, and discovered nothing there, understood that it was all up to her, and she'd never felt more helpless in her life.

She went to the switch by the door and opened the blinds, saw the office half deserted, a handful of account managers at their desks, tucking into Pret. She hadn't thought it was as late as one o'clock, but her watch told her it had just gone ten past. She'd missed Peter's lunch-round, she realised; the blinds had been down, he wouldn't have knocked.

She decided to go out and get some food even though she wasn't at all hungry, needing to escape from the claustrophobic fears, envisioning open air and movement as a nauseous woman might have envisioned a glass of cool fresh water. Picking up her handbag, she walked out through the main office, towards the lifts.

In reception, she had a strong sense that she was being watched, and her head jerked round. Her immediate thought was *Sophie*, but there was nobody there. *You're on edge, Rachel. You need to calm down.* It was true, she was appallingly tense. Her heart had picked up speed in that moment of turning, and wasn't slowing down anywhere near as quickly as it should have done. *Think of relaxing things. Cool fresh water. Cool fresh water.*

She walked and walked, passing Farringdon station and pubs and cafés and jewellery shops, barely aware of the lunchtime crowds and the steady flow of traffic, inexplicably aware of the endless procession of garish signs saluting her through windows. LAST MINUTE DEALS. HOT SALT BEEF. NO APPOINTMENT NECESSARY. *Cool fresh water. Cool fresh water.* In the mêlée of Farringdon Market, she wandered aimlessly through noise and leather jackets and second-hand books, focused on nothing but the meaningless mantra in her head, obscurely reassuring. *Cool fresh water.*

Leaving the market, she had a feeling of being watched again. But as before, when she turned her head, she could see nobody she knew.

She'd done her best to calm down, she realised regretfully, even though she was still a long way from relaxed. All that remained was to get a sandwich and return to her office. She was walking past Starbucks, less than five minutes' walk from the BHN building, when she heard her name being called behind her.

'Rachel?'

She turned. It was Peter.

12

She stopped, and waited for him to reach her. There was something incongruous about the sight of him here, out in the fresh air; that thin, pale face, those closed-off pale-blue eyes. They stood together, and she felt as if time was running at slow-motion speed, dreamlike.

'How are you?' she asked at last.

'I'm all right.' A brief pause. 'I just saw you walking.'

And thought I'd say hi, that was what he should have said next – but nothing came out. The silence between them was stranger than ever, underscored not by air-conditioning, but by the mundane noises of a sunny weekday lunchtime: cars passing, office girls chatting.

'Well,' she said, 'isn't it a lovely day?'

'I suppose so. It always feels the same round here to me. Even in winter.'

He didn't say anything else, seemed to feel no need of conversation. Rachel had no idea how to continue. She thought she wanted to let this strangeness slip away with a casual glance at her watch and a glib excuse, but found she somehow couldn't. Part of her sensed it might never come again, this moment, this opportunity. 'I don't have to head back yet,' she said. 'Want to go for a coffee?'

'Sure. That'd be good.'

In Starbucks, they joined the queue at the counter and didn't speak. She had no idea what he was thinking, what he thought she was. 'What do you want?' he asked abruptly.

The words seemed to carry an infinity of significance, before she realised what he'd meant. Somehow, the anticlimax only seemed to strengthen the tension between them. 'Cappuccino,

69

please,' she said. She watched him relay the order to the counter-hand, get his wallet out. 'Don't worry,' she said, reaching quickly for her own, 'it's on me.'

'It's all right. I'll pay,' he said, and did.

Downstairs, in the main seating area, the bright afternoon ceased to exist. A middle-aged man read yesterday's *Times* in a forest of empty armchairs and little round tables, rosy side lamps, shadows. A Cardigans track played from hidden speakers.

'So where do you live?' she asked him, sitting down. 'With your family, or . . .'

'On my own. I moved out last year,' he said. 'It was the best thing I ever did.'

A long pause stretched out before she spoke again. She felt as if she was in the presence of someone much older than she was, keeping up a steady stream of nervous banalities for fear of a silence she didn't understand. 'Why? Didn't you like it there?'

'With my mother and sister?' No words for long seconds; muted, wailing guitars over the speakers. 'I hated it there. It was hell.'

His words interested her, and she looked at him closely. Again, she was struck by the strangeness of his face, how its edgy, bony look could become almost beautiful in a tiny change of angle, a subtle change of light. 'What was wrong with it?'

'They were there. I like being on my own.'

A flicker of something in his eyes that might or might not have been her imagination – something darting, elusive. She wanted very badly to know what it was. 'Why?'

'It's just how I am. Don't you feel the same?'

The words jolted her. She told herself she shared his isolation not at all, that he'd been mistaken in thinking she did. She shrugged, in a gesture intended to look casual, and hurried to change the subject, move the spotlight off herself. 'So what do you do when you're not working? Got a girlfriend?'

70

'No.' The denial was unequivocal. 'I never wanted one,' he said. 'Not till I met you.'

The remark was offered coldly, and not expanded on at all; she was amazed but somehow *not* amazed, nowhere near as jolted as she knew she should have been. More than ever, she sensed the darkness within him, pulling at her like a magnetic current. Unnerved, she tore away from it with a great effort of will, setting her cup down, checking her watch. Her little noise of shock was only half feigned. 'My God, it's nearly half two. I have to go back.' She rose from the table, and he watched her. 'Well, thanks for the coffee. Expect I'll see you tomorrow.'

She walked upstairs, past the counter, out into the sunshine. The end of their meeting brought a mix of relief and profound disappointment. Having finally spoken to him at length, she felt she knew even less about him than she had done before. The blue window-glass of BHN appeared across the road, and she crossed towards it. It occurred to her that he hadn't asked her a thing about herself throughout their conversation. She walked up the white-stone steps and into the building, trying to brush him from her mind like a symptom of a disease she feared.

13

'Can't wait for the Royal Academy tonight,' said Jessie. It was lunchtime, and they were walking to the sandwich shop. 'It should be excellent.'

'I'm looking forward to it too,' said Sophie. 'We never had anything like that where I used to work.'

'Your old place sounds really grim, if you don't mind me saying.' Sophie shook her head, agreeing. 'How long were you there for?'

Sophie wanted to lie, but somehow couldn't. 'Six years.'

'Jesus.' Jessie stared, frankly aghast. 'How did you stick it?'

'I don't know. Six years – it was just one day at a time. It went by. You know.' It amazed Sophie to realise how true her words were – it was the first time she'd ever expressed them out loud. 'There aren't that many good jobs in Underlyme, unless you're a doctor or a lawyer or something like that. All the ambitious kids moved away after college, and I just – stayed. My friends there all work in cafés and newsagents and things. When we met up, we didn't even talk about how bored we were. It just felt normal.'

'So what made you come here?'

'My dad died. My mum got married again.' She spoke baldly, two simple statements of fact. 'Underlyme looked different after that.'

'God. I'm really sorry.' Sophie made an awkward little sound that could have meant anything. Obviously interpreting it as grief, Jessie hurried to move the conversation on. 'My dad ran off with another woman when I was three. My brother was four. You'd think that'd be too young for things to get to you, but I think it really got to him.'

Again, the rise of interest. Sophie castigated herself for her prurience, but she couldn't stop herself asking. 'How do you mean?'

'He's always been really quiet. Withdrawn. Never had any friends, even at school. Never seemed to want any.' Jessie broke off, sighed. 'Mum always did her best for him, but he never seemed to like her. Or me. Maybe he just doesn't like people.'

'That's a shame.' They went into the sandwich shop, joined the queue. 'Have you got any other brothers or sisters?'

'No. Just Peter,' said Jessie. 'He doesn't live at home any more, though. Moved out last year – some poky little bedsit in Tooting, not that I've ever seen it. Mum couldn't understand why he'd choose *that* over home.' Sophie nodded sympathetically. They were served at the counter, side by side.

'Did I tell you?' asked Jessie, obviously relieved to find a new topic of conversation. 'I'm on reception at quarter to eight. Have you checked the rota yet?'

'Yeah. I'm on at eight.'

'Shouldn't be too bad. Most of the clients should have turned up by then.' Then they were approaching the BHN building, returning to the necessary near-silence of a busy afternoon with the Royal Academy strong in everyone's mind, a Christmas Eve feeling intensifying hour by hour.

By five thirty, the office had already begun to drain empty, and a quick barrage of e-mails appeared concerning the night ahead. *Will everyone please remember that no smoking is permitted in the building. If you are on reception duty, please make sure you are there on time.* 'You ready to go, Soph?' asked Jessie, heading over. 'Leave it for the morning, you might as well.' Then they were leaving together, walking out towards Farringdon station, and whatever the evening might contain.

14

Ten to eight in the Royal Academy, and Jessie was on reception. Sophie walked through an apparently endless maze of interconnecting galleries, alone. The floors were glossy parquet, the walls so white they seemed luminous. Sophie saw knots of people and heard the steady murmur of cocktail-party chatter, felt an airy and civilised impersonality surround her on all sides.

She walked and looked at paintings, glass of champagne in hand, rather enjoying her solitude in this place. She paused for some time in front of a strange grey woman silhouetted against a blood-red sunset, half-decipherable words tangling in a black scrawl like a child's drawing of smoke. She had no idea whether it was in the style of Picasso or Dali or Lucien Freud, but something about it both fascinated and disturbed her. She looked and looked, before the hushed voices of two approaching women brought her back to where she was. 'I mean, come on, Sara, why does it have to be Craig and Neil?' one was complaining. 'She's never led a pitch before, has she?' Sophie moved on quickly, flushed out of her private reverie, the grey woman's image still vivid in her mind.

Checking her watch, she saw it was almost eight o'clock; time she was heading for reception. She made her way back through the labyrinth of galleries, which were considerably louder and more crowded than they'd been when she'd come in with Jessie. Past the tray-holding waiters by the first set of double doors, she walked down the steps, towards the foyer.

She'd anticipated an endless queue of restive clients, impatient for name-badges and champagne, and was startled to see none. Only one other person stood behind the makeshift reception desk, radiating an extrovert's boredom. At first, Sophie couldn't quite place her, then recognition clicked into place. Rachel's erstwhile lift companion; the big redhead with the messy corkscrew curls. She looked round as Sophie approached, obviously glad to have some company.

'Looks like we're doing the graveyard shift, doesn't it?' she said.

'It does, a bit. Where's everyone else?'

'God knows. It was just the same last year – loads of people never showed up for the late shifts. They hardly ever check, you know. Just leave it up to our natural honesty.' The redhead laughed. 'We must be born suckers. I'm Kate Abbott, by the way.'

Sophie smiled back. 'I'm Sophie Townsend.'

'You a mate of Rachel's?'

The question came out of nowhere, and startled Sophie. She hadn't thought she'd been recognised. 'Well – in a way,' she said evasively. 'We sort of grew up together.'

'Old pals from school?'

The murmur of voices from upstairs was the only sound in the world for long seconds.

Sophie took a deep breath. 'She's my cousin,' she said, and wondered when she'd spoken the words last.

15

Andrew stood and looked at the painting. He'd been studying it for some minutes now, but the longer he looked, the most obscurely fascinating he found it – a grey and shadowy female figure silhouetted against a gory sunset, a black scrawl of near-illegible words emerging from the figure's mouth. He couldn't quite pinpoint its resonance in his mind, but it lingered in some dark corner, echoing, troubling him.

Slowly, his concentration began to drift away from it, and he felt the world turning up around him again – the steady, muted roar of a hundred conversations going on at once in these vast high-ceilinged rooms, words caught here and there as people came and went. 'Well, the client went home happy,' someone was saying loudly, in the centre of a group walking past. A couple to his left were deep in conversation. 'I wish I knew how that Fiat pitch is going,' one of them murmured. 'You know, I wanted to work on that myself, and . . .' There was nothing, Andrew thought, more intensely alienating than hearing a group of strangers from another industry talking shop on all sides. He looked at the painting one last time before moving on, wondering why Rachel had asked him here, why he'd agreed to come.

'Andrew – hi!'

A loud voice to his left. He turned. Two women were bearing down on him; one a big, hearty colleague of Rachel's he'd met a few times in the past, the other trailing in her wake almost unwillingly. He didn't recognise her at all, struggling to place the other before remembering – Kate Abbott, of course.

'How's it going?' Kate asked as they reached him. 'Mind if we join you?'

'Christ, no.' He grinned. 'I'd be glad of the company.'

'We just got off reception. Next to nothing to do. Seems like all the clients are here already,' Kate said blithely. 'Suppose Rachel's off with some of them?'

'I think so,' he said. 'Haven't seen her since I got here.'

'Oh well. Suppose it's the price of promotion.'

While Kate seemed entirely comfortable, he noticed that her companion seemed very ill-at-ease, eyes darting nervously over his shoulder. He was surprised Kate hadn't introduced him to the little blonde. 'Hi,' he said, extending a hand. 'I'm Andrew Megson – Rachel's boyfriend.'

'Oh, I'm sorry!' The blonde shook his hand awkwardly, but it was Kate who spoke; the expression of bewilderment looked all wrong on her blunt, open face. 'I thought you knew each other,' and silence fell again, the air between them heavy with incomprehension. 'This is Sophie Townsend,' Kate ploughed on. 'You know, Rachel's cousin.'

For a long second, Andrew looked at her, then back at the blonde. He felt as if he'd walked into a movie half an hour in, but it was worse than that – he *should* know, of course he should. None of them spoke for some time; he struggled to mould a conventional response out of the materials to hand.

'It's great to meet you at last,' he said slowly. 'Surprised we haven't run into each other before.'

'Well, I only came to London last month.' Kate didn't seem to realise how uncomfortable she was, but *he* did – could see her making the best of a situation she didn't want to be in, pretending everything was normal, just like he was. 'Before that, I'd lived in Underlyme all my life. You know, in Dorset.'

Another uncomfortable pause extended, troubled by flickering glances, the sense of three minds trying to see into each other, until it was mercifully broken by the bright, perky voice of a teenage girl with curly fair hair. 'Hi, Soph,' she said, hurrying over. 'Thought you'd got lost or something. Oh, I'm sorry – am I interrupting?'

'Not at all. Don't worry about it.' Sophie turned back to Kate and Andrew apologetically, trying and failing to conceal her relief. 'Well, I'd better go,' she said. 'Nice to meet you, Andrew.'

She walked away beside the other girl. Andrew watched her exit as he'd watched the painting earlier. 'She's really nice,'

Kate was saying from somewhere far away. 'Works in the admin department. I can't believe Rachel never told me about her.' Then the long-lost cousin headed through an archway and disappeared from sight.

16

Rachel strolled through the gallery with Diane and a handful of clients from Fanta. Unable to quite join in with the confidence of Diane's laughter. 'Well, I'm glad you're enjoying yourselves,' Diane was announcing brassily, hundred-watt smile sweeping the room like a searchlight. 'I must say, I've never been much of a one for art – but I do like these get-togethers. It's so much easier to chat outside a boardroom.'

'It's a good idea,' one of the clients replied. 'Surprising more agencies don't have events like this, really.'

'Well – just goes to show that we're the best. You know you're in safe hands with Brent Harvey Nash.' Diane was arch, professional, in her element. Her gaze moved to Rachel. 'Wouldn't you agree, Rach?'

'Sure would.' She thought Diane was looking at her oddly. She'd been uncharacteristically subdued all night, couldn't help it. The Fiat pitch gnawed and rustled in the shadows, and suddenly, she wanted very badly to be alone. 'Back in a minute. Just going to the loo.'

She walked, gradually picking up speed, through gallery after gallery, the noise deafening now, roaring in her ears like the sound of the sea in an open shell. Feeling panic terribly close. *Cool fresh water*, and the creative briefing first thing tomorrow, and the stacks of Fiat paperwork on her desk. The nightmare feeling of helplessness. *Cool fresh water*, and a thousand champagne flutes en route to a thousand mouths, and a thousand conversations all going on at once – the sense of drowning in something bigger than the world, a tiny speck, adrift and struggling—

She saw Andrew talking to Kate, and wanted very badly to pretend she hadn't seen them, keep walking to the Ladies', to a closed cubicle and a place to clear her mind. But it was no good. They'd seen her, she'd have to go over.

'Hi, Kate.' She struggled for calm, businesslike confidence in her voice, her eyes, her thoughts. 'Hi, Andrew. Sorry I've been ignoring you, but I'm stuck with the Fanta people. They probably won't stay long.'

'Don't worry about it.' She'd spoken to Andrew, but it was Kate who answered. In a second, she became aware of something strange in their scrutiny. 'By the way, Rach – didn't know you had a cousin working here.'

At first, Rachel literally didn't understand – *what's she talking about, some kind of weird joke?* – then realisation crashed down. 'Well, in a way,' she heard herself saying, 'but we've never been close. You've met her?'

'We were on reception together, got chatting. Introduced her to Andrew,' said Kate, then, her casual tone becoming one of enquiry, 'Why didn't you tell me?'

A terrifying sense of the walls closing in around her. Rachel stood in bright, cold panic, feeling something close to hatred for Kate's unthinking security. Kate carried on, oblivious to Andrew's bewilderment, to Rachel's own desperation. 'Looks like even Andrew didn't know. You're a dark horse all right, Rach.'

Rachel couldn't think of anything to say, but the silence between them screamed to be broken. She was very aware of Andrew's eyes on her. 'There's nothing much to tell,' she said quickly. 'She's just, you know, someone I grew up with. There's nothing *secret* about it.'

Her distracted tone struck a wrong note that she caught too clearly. Suddenly, she was aware of nothing but the enormity of all she was denying: a sunny garden, a long hot summer, a secret that had almost destroyed her life. 'I've got to go,' she said, distraught, 'I've got to go to the loo. The clients will wonder where I am,' and she was hurrying away, feeling eyes fixed on her back, the ground falling away before her.

17

'Well, I'm up for it,' Jessie was saying. 'It's not ten o'clock yet. Could do with a good night out.'

Conversation had begun to fade around them, and the gallery was slowly emptying. Standing with Jessie and a few people she knew from Accounts, Sophie cut in quickly. 'I think I'll go home. I feel a bit tired, to be honest.'

'Are you sure? It should be a good laugh.' Jessie looked at her, concerned. 'You look a bit pale, you know. Are you okay?'

'Oh, I'm fine. Really.' Much as she liked Jessie, the prospect of this noisy, anonymous evening extending indefinitely filled Sophie with terror. She very much wanted to be alone with her thoughts. 'Have a good time, okay? I'll see you in the morning.'

Sophie walked away from the little group quickly. She feared an encounter with Rachel, but, walking through the maze of galleries, she saw nobody she knew. Reception was deserted now, the long table bare. A little group of smokers stood outside, watching her leave with bored strangers' eyes.

It was odd, the way she felt; less like thinking than trying to untangle intricate knots in her mind, at first impatiently, then with resigned and infinite care. She remembered that uncomfortable conversation earlier – the almost telepathic sense of Andrew's bewilderment, Kate's unawareness. It had been like walking through a minefield, having no idea what innocent remark would catch Rachel out in a lie. Without knowing exactly why, she was a hundred per cent sure that Rachel *had* lied to both friend and boyfriend about her past life, or, at least, hadn't told them certain parts of it. Sophie was far from sure that she blamed her.

Still, it was a shame that she'd had to evade like that. She'd liked Andrew. There was something about him that, in a different situation, she would have warmed to.

The strangest thing of all about tonight had been remembering what she and Rachel really were to each other. Of course, she'd always known and would always know, but at some instinctive level, the knowledge had slipped out of sight; fallen, unnoticed, dusty with years of neglect. Ever since that fateful summer, it had been easy to forget she was related to the Carters. Afterwards, the two families had had next to nothing to do with each other.

Now she came to think of it, her mother and Nina hadn't even been close *before* those events. She and Rachel had become friends on their own, less because of than in spite of parental pressure. In a small town like Underlyme, family ties were set in stone – it was considered bizarre that first cousins could attend the same school and have little more than a nodding acquaintance with each other. Still, that was all she and Rachel had had, in the beginning – no sense of shared blood had united them. They'd said hi in corridors and playgrounds, but they'd lived in different worlds.

Her mother, frowning by the sink, washing up after a phone call. *Well, I can't say I approve of the way my sister lives. Every child needs a father . . .*

For the first eight years of her life, Sophie remembered, the family tie had consisted of uncomfortable short visits, maybe two or three in the average year. *We're having the Carters for lunch, next Sunday.* She'd hated those visits, able even at that age to identify various sources of tension – Nina's thinly veiled dislike of Brian Townsend, his equally obvious disapproval of Nina. A sense of Linda Townsend standing behind her husband and nodding whenever he spoke. It seemed that any conversation could take a dangerous turn towards argument; a harmless news story could easily lead Brian off on a Family Values sermon, while Nina bit her tongue hard. Linda in Laura Ashley and Nina in tie-dye, two sisters who seemed to have nothing in common beyond an accident of birth.

Strange that Sophie and Rachel should have become best friends in spite of those circumstances. But they had done . . .

Out of Kentish Town station, the night was dark and very empty. The quick walk back to the shared house held too many shadows. Inside, one of the pleasant strangers was coming downstairs, and brief smiles and greetings were exchanged as they passed each other. Preparing for bed quickly, Sophie lay awake for some time, not wanting to remember any more of the past.

18

'I can't believe you never told me about her,' Andrew was saying. 'After all, she's your cousin.'

'Look, I told you. It's not important.' Andrew parked, turned off the engine. Rachel got out of the passenger seat, slamming the door behind her a little too hard. 'I just don't see why it matters.'

'She's your *cousin*. She's family.' They walked towards the main doors of the apartment building. 'You know, you've never really told me anything about your family. Just your mother.'

'I don't have other family. Not any more.' As they stepped into the foyer, Rachel was making an immense effort to stay calm. 'I haven't spoken to any of the Townsends in years. They're just not part of my life these days.'

'That's a shame.' He unlocked the door to their flat. 'Why not get back in touch? We could have Sophie round for dinner one night, invite some of my friends too. Make it a little party.'

Rachel felt the colour drain from her face as she walked in behind him. The idea was like a scene from a nightmare. 'I just don't want to,' she said harshly. 'All right?'

The door swung shut. He turned to look at her closely. 'Rachel, what's the matter?'

'Nothing's the matter. I just don't want her here.' Her previous vehemence had shocked her, and she spoke with calm, deliberate rationality. 'Do you want to use the bathroom first?'

He sounded puzzled. 'All yours.'

In the bathroom, she closed the door behind her as she always did, and plunged her face into ice-cold water, longing for it to wake her up. But of course, it didn't. This was real, this was happening. The person she was most afraid of in the world had somehow forced entry into her new life.

It had been the sunny openness of Andrew's personality that had drawn her to him. But suddenly, she found it at once maddening and deeply alienating, as if the distance between them had only just become apparent. He literally didn't know about the darkness she'd escaped from, had no idea it existed. And she felt him become different in her mind, her love for him intensifying even as it took on a sharp edge of terror, as if he belonged to some separate, superior species she could never aspire to, that she yearned after, and didn't understand at all.

Her thoughts turned of their own accord to Peter, and she shivered.

In the bedroom, she set the alarm and turned the light out. When Andrew came in, he got straight into bed beside her. He reached out to touch her breast. She flinched away. 'Don't,' she said quickly. 'Just. Don't. Not tonight.'

He didn't speak after that; she sensed his bewilderment beside her for minutes on end, before it gave way to heavier breathing, then to gentle snores. Rachel had never felt less like sleeping in her life. On the bedside clock, red digital numbers ticked away like the countdown to a movie bomb, inexorably approaching 07:00.

19

She came into the kitchen at seven thirty the following morning, showered and dressed and made-up for work as always. Andrew was reading the morning paper at the table, absently munching Nutella on toast. As she entered, he looked up sharply.

'Morning,' he said. 'Want some breakfast?'

'Thanks, but I haven't got time. I'm giving a briefing at nine sharp – I can't be late.' It was, she thought, as if he watched a vaguely suspicious passer-by from a safe distance. She wondered exactly how much damage had been done the night before. More from habit than anything else, she replaced the jar of Nutella in the cupboard, wiped the counter clean. 'Better go,' she said. 'See you later.'

Out of the flat, there was a fresh, straight-out-of-the-fridge quality to the air that Rachel barely noticed. Her exhaustion was so intense that it didn't even register as exhaustion – a ragged edge to her nerves, a slight change to the look of everything. 'And we're heading for a belting summer here in the capital,' the DJ announced matily from the radio, and she was heading for an amber light, slowing slightly, wondering whether to run through it or not in a horrible moment of indecision; speeding up again, hammering through on red as horns blared around her.

In the BHN reception, she walked over to the lifts, got into one, alone. As the doors shut, the mirrored walls showed her a pale reflection with shadowed, anxious eyes. She reached into her bag, applied more bronzer quickly, with a kind of desperation.

At nine o'clock, Sara and Christina arrived in her office, and at ten past, Craig and Neil did – laid-back in jeans and sweaters, not seeming to care about anything. Rachel briefed them as Sara and Christina listened. 'So, like I said, they're looking for award-winning work,' she concluded. 'Cost's not going to be an issue.'

'You mean, we can really have some fun with this one?' The creatives' air of half-drugged ennui had vanished – they leant forward eagerly, elbows on sketch-pads, sketch-pads on knees. 'Come up with some seriously on-the-edge shit?'

'Sure,' said Rachel briskly. 'It's what they're looking for.'

A brief silence fell; it was Sara who leaned forward this time, lowering her voice. 'I don't know, Rachel. Didn't the head of marketing say he didn't want anything too wacky?'

'Yeah.' Christina joined in, also speaking as if she didn't want the creatives to overhear her. 'Not cool ads for the sake of cool ads, wasn't that what he said in the meeting? Only stuff that really says something about them as a company, he said, and—'

'Well, of course. We all know *that*.' She spoke too sharply, and too quickly, addressing Craig and Neil. 'Of course, we're not looking for another Pot Noodle campaign. Anything too wacky would be way off brief.' And she watched them all looking at her, wondering if they'd noticed the glaring change of gear, knowing they must have.

When the meeting was over and she was alone in her office, she sat unmoving at her desk for some time, staring at a blank computer screen. Trying to rein in a new and immediate fear. A significant part of her mind had doubted her ability to lead this pitch from the start, but now it was more than doubt or paranoia. Her fears had something tangible to feed on. She'd either misinterpreted or completely forgotten a key part of the brief, and if Sara and Christina hadn't cut in, Craig and Neil would have set to work on entirely the wrong kind of concepts.

Of course I hadn't forgotten what the head of marketing said, she reassured herself frantically. *It's just last night, Andrew. I can't think straight this morning.* Far from distracting her from her worries regarding Fiat, the events at the Royal Academy had only driven them further home – like two noises running on at once, each trying to drown the other out.

At twelve noon, there was a knock at the door. 'Come in,' she called.

Peter stepped in. The door swung slowly shut behind him. 'Hi, Rachel,' he said. 'Want anything from Pret?'

As often, recently, she didn't know quite how to look at him; wondered what he might be thinking, was very aware how little she knew about it. 'Sushi deluxe, please,' she said. 'Nothing else.'

Silence again as he jotted her order down. Taut, charged silence, stronger than ever before. He stood and looked at her for a second. Behind her desk, she sat and looked back.

He said at last, 'Do you want to come out for a drink sometime?'

She had no idea what to say, heard the words come out on their own. 'I have a boyfriend, you know. We live together.'

Something flickered in his eyes, but she didn't think it was embarrassment. More than ever, she longed to know what it was that came and went like a restless trespasser in that expressionless face.

'Just to talk. Nothing else,' he said. 'I like being with you. I feel like I know you.'

For some time she didn't say a thing, and he observed her silence as intently as he'd observed her words. 'Well,' she said at last, 'why not?'

'There's a pub up the Christchurch Road – the Turk's Head. About ten minutes' walk from here.' She knew where it was, nodded her awareness before he spoke again. 'What about meeting in there next Wednesday night?'

'I could come out for an hour or so.' She couldn't quite believe she was speaking the words, and told herself harshly that her acceptance was in no way a betrayal of Andrew. Through the glass panel, she saw a familiar world with the sound switched off – Kate typing busily at her computer, Sara walking over to the printer. 'How does six thirty sound?'

'Sounds good,' he said. 'I'll see you there.'

When he'd gone, her anxiety deepened. She could see Peter's darkness as clearly as she'd ever seen anything, and still she felt it pull at her – a hitherto unsuspected kinship, alienation recognising itself across a crowded room. She moved her eyes quickly to the photograph on her desk. A neat square of blinding white sunlight fell across the smiling faces, and as she looked at them, she felt jolted; as if she'd taken a small but crucial step away from that world, saw it become more beautiful, less attainable, less real.

20

'Just going for a sandwich, Ed. If anyone calls, can you take a message?'

'Sure thing. See you in a bit.'

Andrew rose from his desk, headed through the rugby scrum of the busy office. 'There's a fax here from Leo at Goldman Sachs,' someone was yelling. 'Who's expecting a fax from—' Then the door was swinging shut behind him. He stood and waited for a lift to arrive, all the time thinking about Rachel.

How unbelievably weird last night had been. Rachel's near-pathological secrecy concerning her family, her apparent terror of her cousin. Then the Dr Jekyll of her sexual personality manifesting itself yet again. He couldn't understand it at all. While it didn't matter to him whether she had a cousin or not, the sheer abnormality of her concealment meant far too much, a tiny detail giving scale to a blank white space in his mind. He'd been measuring in inches, but the map was drawn in miles.

It wasn't just that he didn't know her exact family tree. When it came to the things that really mattered, he didn't know anything about her.

Why hadn't she told him that she worked with Sophie? It was a riddle to him, repeating endlessly in his thoughts as he walked to the sandwich shop. He'd asked her and asked her last night, and she'd refused point-blank to answer. She didn't just keep her secrets hidden. It was as if she had them under lock and key, jealously guarded twenty-four hours a day.

But he couldn't stand this new uncertainty. That morning, in the kitchen with her, he'd known it for a fact, and reeled before the extent of his own ignorance. Could anyone really live with bewilderment this intense – fall asleep every night beside a total stranger, make meaningless small talk with that stranger every morning, spend weekends and holidays and possibly a lifetime with a woman you didn't know at all? His parents' easy, conventional togetherness had set the benchmark for long-term relationships in his mind. Whatever he had with Rachel now seemed appallingly flimsy, a grotesque caricature of love.

Before last night, it had been unnerving. Today, it horrified him.

As he went back to work, he realised abruptly that there was only one thing for it. He wasn't entirely comfortable with the prospect, and there could be no pretending that he was – it was too close to spying, sneaking around behind her back – but it seemed there was no alternative. Only one possible way to salvage their relationship, to find some key to her real self. A kind of psychological chemotherapy, the ultimate last resort . . .

Back through the office, he sat down at his desk. 'No messages,' Ed announced from the next desk. Andrew murmured preoccupied thanks and opened his wallet. Extracting Rachel's business card, he looked for the central switchboard number he'd never dialled before in his life; pressed it out quickly, receiver held tightly to his ear.

The voice came down the line after the second ring. 'Good afternoon, Brent Harvey Nash.'

'Hi,' he said. 'Could you put me through to the admin department?'

21

Sophie was in the middle of some filing when the phone rang on her desk. She picked it up without thinking twice about it. 'Hello?'

'Hello – is that Sophie?'

'Yes.' She didn't recognise the male voice. 'Who's this?'

'It's Andrew. Rachel's boyfriend.'

Sophie couldn't have been much more surprised if her caller had identified himself as the Prince of Wales. He carried on quickly. 'Look, I'm sorry to bother you – I expect you're busy – but I'd really like to talk to you about Rachel. To be honest, I'm a bit worried about her.'

She couldn't think of anything to say. The voice was embarrassed, determined. 'Is there any way you could meet me for lunch one day next week? I can come and meet you in Farringdon.'

Shock made it impossible to think of an excuse, and long seconds of silence seemed to last full minutes. She had to say something, and the words jumped out on their own. 'Well, okay.'

'That's great.' She couldn't believe she'd just agreed, heard his relief with mounting horror. 'How about Monday lunch-time? Would that be all right for you?'

'I suppose so.' More than anything, she wanted to tell him she'd changed her mind, but she couldn't, there was no possible way of phrasing it. 'I won't be able to stay more than half an hour, mind,' she said quickly. 'It's really busy here.'

'That's fine. How about meeting at one o'clock at the All Bar One near you?'

'All right.'

The words were ungracious, she knew, but she *felt* ungracious, apprehensive, resentful. Off the phone, she found she couldn't concentrate on the filing. Over and over, she wondered how she'd possibly got shanghaied into *this*. The last person in the world she wanted to talk about was Rachel, she thought, and remembered last night at the Royal Academy with a mental shudder.

But it was too late to back out now. Returning to the day's work, she forced herself to think philosophically. He couldn't exactly get the thumbscrews out. She didn't have to tell him anything at all. But a sense of worry still lingered, nibbling at the edges of her mind with sharp rodent teeth; an overwhelming feeling that she'd made the wrong decision when she'd accepted.

22

When Rachel's key turned in the lock, the door swung open to pitch-black silence. She locked it behind her, and turned the hallway light on quickly.

For the sake of something to do, she made a start on the dinner, getting the ingredients out of the fridge, peeling potatoes at the sink. She hadn't put the radio on, and when the phone shrieked in the hallway, the sound was as heart-stopping as a tinkle of broken glass. The knife slipped in her hand, slicing her forefinger up the side.

'*Shit.*' She put the finger in her mouth, sucked hard. Tearing off a sheet of kitchen paper, she wrapped it round the cut quickly, hurried out into the hallway and picked up the receiver.

'Hi, Rachel. It's me.'

'Mum. How are you?'

'Oh, I'm fine. Met Linda for lunch today, in that little café by Smith's. Kelly's, or something. You know the one.'

'Oh, yes. How is she?'

'She's fine. To be honest, she's still a bit prim and proper for my liking – but so much nicer than when she was married to that Brian.' The name hit Rachel like an electric shock, affecting her like it hadn't done in years. Nina carried on blithely. 'You know, she's still in touch with his family. I could never really understand that. It was like she adopted them as soon as they got married.'

'I know,' said Rachel. 'I remember.'

'I suppose she just wanted a family of her own.' Nina's voice was reflective. 'It's weird, you know, how things like that affect you. Growing up in those foster homes didn't bother me at all, they were all nice enough people. But Linda – you know how she's always wanted a *normal* sort of life.'

'What did she say?' Rachel asked, then, quickly, 'Did she mention Sophie?'

'Only to say she's found a job. To be honest, I think that's the last Linda's going to hear from her for a while – sad, really.' Nina took a deep breath, then spoke again, brightly. 'So how's work going? Any more promotions on the cards?'

Out of nowhere, Rachel was reminded of the Fiat pitch. It was like being thrown into freezing water on a Sunday-morning stroll, and she struggled not to betray her fear. 'It's going great. I'm enjoying it.'

'I'm glad. You know, I'm so proud of you, Rachel. You're doing fantastically well – you're going to have a great future in that agency.'

The crushing weight of love and expectation – it was as terrible as it had been all those years ago, and worse. The impossibility of confessing the truth, inflicting that kind of disappointment on someone who meant so much to you. Now, as then, Rachel couldn't do it, and forced herself to speak cheerfully, her tone palpably insincere to her own ears. 'Well, thanks. I hope so.'

'I'm sure of it,' said Nina, then, 'I suppose I'd better let you go. You must have dinner to cook, or is it Andrew's turn tonight?'

'My turn,' said Rachel. 'Speak to you soon. Have a good evening.'

'You too. Love to Andrew.'

Rachel hung up, seeing the makeshift bandage on her finger

as though for the first time. She hurried into the bathroom and unwrapped it. It wasn't a bad cut, she saw, she'd just need a plaster. She went to the cupboard and got one out, dressing her finger carefully. As she smoothed the plaster down, her composure collapsed like a house of cards, leaving nothing but sheer terror. She was leaning over the washbasin, tears running down her cheeks on to polished porcelain, the only sound a hoarse, racked string of guttural noises that didn't sound like crying at all.

When the tears had tailed off, she raised her face slowly to look at her reflection. A red-eyed apparition with black-streaked cheeks stared back apprehensively from the glass. *Andrew could be back any minute. He can't see me like this.* Appalled, she got her make-up bag, bolted the bathroom door behind her. Meeting her own gaze in the mirror, she reconstructed herself with painstaking care; creating the woman who belonged here like a picture drawn from memory.

By the time Andrew got home, dinner was ready, and she was real again.

23

Sophie was amazed how quickly Monday morning passed. Usually, she'd glance at the clock across the office to see ten minutes had gone by. Today, it was more like half an hour. As lunchtime approached, the idea of not meeting Andrew became more and more seductive in her mind, and by twelve noon, it had become an almost irresistible temptation.

But she knew she'd have to go. She had no possible way of getting in touch and making an excuse, and she guessed he'd be travelling considerably out of his way. It wouldn't be fair to just leave him waiting there, not when she'd said she'd meet him . . .

At twenty to one, Jessie stopped by her desk. 'Coming for lunch, Soph?'

'I can't, sorry. I'm meeting someone at one.'

'Anyone interesting?'

'Just a friend.' She lied to simplify rather than confuse, to trim the ragged edges off the situation. 'Someone I know from home.'

'Oh, well – have a nice time. See you later.'

Sitting at her desk, Sophie watched her leave, watched the office clock move slowly past twelve forty-five; it was no good, she realised, she'd have to go now. She rose from her seat and got the lift down to reception. Squares of sunlight fell across fake marble and green pot-plants, and soothed her not at all. How much she'd prefer to be walking to the sandwich shop with Jessie. She went through the revolving doors like a condemned woman approaching the electric chair.

Inside, All Bar One was chaos, and the bar was packed. Pushing her way through the crowds, she saw Andrew standing alone, further down. She made her way towards him.

'Hi, Sophie. Glad you could make it.' They had to raise their voices considerably to make themselves heard. 'What would you like to drink?'

'A white wine spritzer, please.' Standing by the bar, they watched the frantic industry behind it for a few awkward seconds. 'God, it's busy in here,' she said at last. 'Like being on the tube.'

'Do you want to sit down when we finally get served? We'll have to get a table to eat, anyway.'

'That would be nice,' she said, and heard the falsity of her own tone too clearly – a necessary-small-talk voice, loud, cheery and hollow.

Andrew was served, paid. They pushed through the crowd again, to the slightly less-populated area between packed bar and packed tables. 'Let's just keep our eyes peeled,' he said. 'Someone's got to leave *eventually*.'

'Well, I hope so. I've never been in here before.' Neither spoke for long seconds, before she spotted movement across the room. 'Oh, hang on, you're right. They're getting up over there.'

They hurried over to the newly vacated table and sat down, faced each other across it with embarrassed social smiles. A waitress handed them menus. 'The food's not too bad in these places,' he said, as she walked away. 'Personally, I'd recommend the cod.'

'I might try it.' It was like the comments before a job interview began in earnest – the weight of the future hung uncertainly between them. 'Are you going to have a starter?'

'No, but feel free. I'm glad you agreed to come out.'

The waitress returned, asked if they were ready to order yet. 'Well, *I'm* going to have the cod,' he said. 'What about you?'

'I'll have the same,' she said, and the waitress left.

'So,' Andrew said at last. 'You and Rachel grew up in Underlyme.'

She'd known it could come at any second. 'That's right.'

'What's it like there? I've never been.'

Why not ask Rachel? The words rose in her throat and she forced them back, realising how paranoid and unreasonable they sounded. 'It's a nice little town,' she said. 'Not so little, really. It just feels that way when you live there.'

'You both went to school there?'

A sharp edge entered her voice. 'Of course. Where else?'

'Were you close, growing up?'

God, I don't want to talk about this. She forced on Lisa Shah's professional manner like a too-tight shoe, Lisa Shah's smile. 'I suppose so, yes,' she said. 'We were friends.'

'Look – I don't really know how to ask this, but I've been wondering. Did anything happen to her, back in Underlyme?' His hands moved in a gesture of helpless eloquence. 'Christ, I know that's not very specific, but I don't really know what I'm looking for. It just feels like she's not telling me something.'

A sunny garden and a long hot summer; Acacia Avenue, the past. The world pressed in around Sophie as if tightened by screws – the echoing noise, the slight breeze from the rotating overhead paddles, the besuited crowds pressing round the bar.

93

When she spoke, she was amazed at the composure of her own voice. 'Look, I'm really sorry, but if you want to talk about things like that, you should ask Rachel. I feel all wrong, talking behind her back.'

She watched him. He watched her. 'When you called, I didn't know what you meant. Not really,' she said. 'I shouldn't have agreed to come. I'm sorry.'

'It's all right,' he said quietly. 'It's my fault.'

The silence that followed was more awkward than ever. The waitress returned with their food. 'Thanks,' said Andrew, then, to Sophie, 'Hey, might as well have a good lunch anyway. No point just sitting in silence, is there?'

She smiled her first genuine smile of the day. Part of her felt absurdly grateful to him for understanding, for trying to salvage something from this tense and fruitless meeting. 'Well,' she said, 'I suppose it makes sense.'

They talked about his job and her job and music and movies. At first it felt strained and unnatural, and she found herself analysing his every remark for traces of Rachel. But gradually it began to seem normal and even pleasant, a relaxing lunch with an amiable and amusing companion. When the waitress came to take their plates, she checked her watch, was amazed to see it was ten past two. 'Oh my God,' she said. 'I'm really sorry, but I'll have to run. I'll be late back.'

'Don't worry about it. Just go,' he said. 'I'll get the bill. It's been good to meet you properly.'

'You too. Thanks a lot, Andrew.'

Back in the office, nobody seemed to notice she was late, and she plunged back into her work gratefully, a little light-headed. Amazing, she thought, she'd had a really nice time after all. It occurred to her that she liked Andrew very much, and found herself wishing she could meet him again.

24

Two thirty on Tuesday afternoon. Rachel sat at her computer, going over some of the Fiat paperwork. She'd been doing it all day, and it had begun to look incomprehensible in the sunlight, words losing meaning as they did when you looked at them too long – *marketing, figures, spend* – becoming a foreign language, a nonsensical collection of syllables before her eyes.

Give yourself a break. This isn't doing any good, you're chasing yourself round in circles. Her eyes moved from the sheaf of papers to the glass partition, and she watched a silent movie world – Kate tapping away at an e-mail, Diane hurrying out to some meeting, Sara and Christina gossiping at their desks. And the longer she looked, the more she felt them become anonymous, draining of resonance as the printed word had. The photograph smiled out at her from her desk, reminding her of Peter, their planned evening together, tomorrow night.

She realised she was biting her nails for the first time in eleven years.

Book Three

I can't believe it.

Keep thinking, this can't be real. I'll wake up any second and it'll be this morning, and nothing'll have happened after all – I'll be about to tell her, then I'll tell her, and everything's going to be okay.

But I know I'm not dreaming. I'd never imagine things this bad.

She was on the swing this morning, when I came out into the garden with my courage screwed right up to tell her. She was reading a magazine.

I've got something to tell you, I said.

She looked up, saw me. What? she said.

It's a secret, I said, but I could see she didn't really understand, tried to make her see how serious this was in my voice. Not just the usual kind, I said. You can't let anyone know I told you.

I looked round, saw the kitchen windows were all wide open. I was scared they'd hear me. Come behind the shed, I said. I'll tell you there.

She still didn't understand. I could tell from the breathless way she ran after me, not giggling, but like she wanted to. Like she thought I was going to tell her who Kathy fancied, or what Justine was saying about Debbie behind her back. But she wasn't going to hear anything like that. Not today.

So we went behind the shed and sat down on the grass, and I told her everything. At first, I wasn't sure I could say it. But when I got started I could feel it all flooding out of me, I didn't even have to think. Like throwing up. And when I finished, I felt just like I'd finished throwing up. This weird sort of relief. An empty feeling.

I looked at her. I'd been looking at the grass by my hand the whole time I'd been talking, and didn't know what to expect. She didn't look horrified or scared like I'd thought she would. Just blank. Her eyes had got big and sort of glassy, staring.

Well? I said. It was a stupid thing to say. I just wanted to know what she was thinking right now, so badly. Aren't you going to say anything?

And then she jumped up. Never knew anyone's face could change so quickly. Sort of hardened and closed at the same time. I always thought it was just something people said, my heart sank. *But that was just how it felt. Could feel it falling inside me like a lift going down twenty floors in a second.*

You're lying, she screamed, and then I was watching her back while she ran away.

I was going to go after her, but something stopped me. Just stood and looked as she ran round the side of the shed. A few seconds later, I heard the back door slam. I could hear everything getting louder all round me. Bees, someone's lawnmower, a radio playing next door. And I suddenly thought of how I'd imagined this as a last resort, IN CASE OF EMERGENCY BREAK GLASS, but I'd just broken the glass and nothing had happened. She'd just run away. She'd still be going away tomorrow.

And the worst thing of all was, I could tell she'd believed me. She hadn't wanted to believe me, but that's different. She'd just blocked it, like putting your hand over your eyes at the scary bit of a horror movie. She'd looked away, and pretended she couldn't hear.

I didn't hate her before.

I hate her now.

1

He hated them.

The one in the office of her own, with the too-blonde, carefully sculpted hair that never moved an inch. Maybe forty-two. A little red-painted doll's mouth and eyes like cold water. She made him think of the kind of music, the kind of perfumes his sister liked. When she was young, she would have giggled like her.

'I'll have the vegetarian sushi,' she was saying. 'Nothing else.'

Back in the main office, he stopped by another. 'The roast pork sandwiches,' she said, 'and the chocolate fudge cake.' A loud, big, red-haired girl, all confidence and freckles and hairy arms, the kind whose voice had risen in the school corridors so you could make it out even in the lunchtime noise. Friendly to everyone but him. Not that he cared.

'And a strawberry smoothie,' she said, returning to an e-mail. A second's glimpse gave him part of it. *Julie says she wants to dump him but when I saw her yesterday she said . . .* He turned away without interest – seeing, recording, indifferent.

The ones who always sat and talked together, the youngish ones; one golden head, the other shiny red. He looked at them and saw emptiness behind polished shells, well-oiled machinery that enabled them to do what had to be done. 'The pasta salad,' one said curtly, and the other immediately tinkled like glass. 'I can't *believe* you're having that again,' she shrilled. 'Do you *know* how many calories are in those?' Then she turned to him, curt as her clone. 'The sushi.' He jotted, turned, heard their voices again behind him. 'Seriously, Sara, do you *know* how high-fat that salad is? I thought you were supposed to be on a *diet*.' He walked out, into the lift, through reception, carrying his hatred like a weapon.

It was everywhere he looked, in the melting afternoon – the shrieking groups outside pubs and wine bars, clustered round ashtrays, pints and Bacardi Breezers. He didn't need to hear them to know the kind of thing they talked about. It was why he lived in their world as little as possible; it had always looked the same to him, ever since he could remember.

In Pret, he was served quickly – the familiar transaction separate from the busy tills, over in seconds. He stepped out into the sunlight with a wicker basket in one hand, walking with a new preoccupation. The only office that mattered had been empty when he'd left, but might be occupied now. The woman he was meeting tomorrow night had become all that mattered.

He knew what love meant now.

2

Rachel and Andrew were eating a quiet dinner in the kitchen. There were too many silences, she thought. She saw his preoccupied expression, and it disturbed her all over again – it was too easy to trace it back to source. Since that evening at the Royal Academy, every evening they'd spent together had felt like this.

'Oh, I forgot to tell you,' he said. 'We got a postcard from Helen this morning.'

Despite herself, she was immensely relieved that he'd spoken. 'Oh, good. How is she?'

'I'll go and get it. It came right after you left for work.'

He went out into the hallway. She thought he'd meant that *he'd* got a postcard from Helen, but when he came back in and handed it to her, she saw it had been addressed to both of them. She read through it quickly as he sat back down and started eating again. 'Well,' she said at last, laying it to one side, 'sounds like she's having a nice time.'

'I don't know. I think she'd sound a bit more enthusiastic if she really was.' He spoke thoughtfully, slightly dubiously. 'I can't see it suiting her for long. She likes her home comforts as much as I do – whatever she thinks, she's not cut out to be a backpacker.'

No matter how Rachel racked her brain, she could find nothing else to say on the subject. Maybe three minutes passed without a word being spoken. 'So,' she said at last, with bright desperation, 'how was work?'

'Oh, fine. Just the usual.' He looked at her across the table. There was something all wrong in his scrutiny, too close, as if he was searching her face. 'What about you? Got anything to tell me about?'

Sudden panic gripped her, a conviction that he was talking about the Fiat pitch. She forced it back. 'Much the same,' she said. 'Nothing to report.'

'Hasn't it changed at all, now you've been promoted? You know, you've hardly told me a thing about it.'

Sara and Christina and work piling up on her desk, a constant image of Diane waiting out of sight. Her composure felt like a heavy object dangling from a fraying rope. 'There's nothing to tell. I'm just a bit busier these days.' The phone shrilled in the hallway, and she was out of her seat in half a second, her heatbeat loud and fast in her ears.

It was for Andrew. He hurried out to take the call as she sat back down at the table. Through the half-open door, she could hear snatches of his conversation – 'Well of course I'm on for the game next Monday night,' he was saying. 'Aren't I usually?' – could see his shadow in the hallway. His fingers were pulling the kinks out of the phone cord in an edgy, preoccupied reflex that wasn't like him at all. Suddenly she wanted more than anything to know what he was thinking, and at the same time, she longed not to.

She reached for Helen's postcard on the table, looked at the round, extroverted schoolgirl writing and the words it spelt out. *Rachel Carter and Andrew Megson.* More than ever, Rachel felt the warmth of inclusion, and it carried terror in its wake. The world that existed beyond it was taking on an extra dimension as she watched, stepping out of a half-forgotten nightmare, becoming real all over again. *And you're looking for it, Rachel. Why else are you meeting Peter tomorrow night? You know you're going to go, and you know you're going to tell Andrew you have to work late, and you know it's what you want. But if it's really what you want, why the hell are you so scared of it?*

But she didn't want to think about that. It was a compulsion as irresistible as the lure of the promenade shelter had been all those years ago. Peter unsettled her deeply, but he also fascinated her, and issues of willpower simply ceased to exist where he was concerned – a weak arm wrestling a stronger one, a swimmer struggling against a lethal current. She was being drawn in by something outside herself.

She grabbed hold of the world around her like a lifebelt – the well-lit kitchen, the cooking smells, Andrew's shadow in the hallway. 'Well, okay,' he was saying, 'send it to me on the e-mail and I'll have a read.' Her eyes fixed once again on Helen's postcard, and she reached out to touch it. In a slow, swooning moment, her life contracted to become a single image – bitten pink-rimmed nails on round schoolgirl's writing, words from another world smiling out between her fingers.

3

Andrew lay awake, pretending to sleep. Wondering what the time was. He couldn't see the clock without sitting up in bed and looking over Rachel's shoulder, and if he did that, he was pretty sure he'd wake her up. Her breathing was quiet, but he could hear it, slightly too quick, slightly too shallow. Nothing like the breathing of deep sleep.

Why don't you just look anyway? he thought. *Even if she does wake up, it's not the end of the world* – but that led him straight back to what he didn't want to face. He didn't want her to wake up because he had no idea what to say to her. Over the last few days, that feeling had become stronger and stronger, escalating with the terrifying speed of forest fire; hundreds of possible words shrivelling before his eyes, leaving nothing but office conversation, lift conversation.

If she woke up, she'd say *what's the matter?* and he'd say *nothing, I just woke up.* And there'd be literally nothing else to talk about.

It was driving him crazy, this tense, uncertain state of affairs. It was like nothing he'd known before. He remembered Tim's phone call earlier. Of course, he hadn't been able to tell Tim about the important things, with Rachel in the kitchen, but lying awake in the too-neat darkness, stark realisation surfaced. He couldn't have discussed them even if Rachel had been miles away, even though Tim was one of his oldest friends; he couldn't imagine himself putting his anxiety into words.

Andrew had never realised before how much of life could be unspeakable, undiscussable – how much he'd been taking for granted for the last twenty-eight years. It had never occurred to him that his confidence was anything but normal; his life was open to viewing by anyone who cared to look. Suddenly, however, he opened his eyes to a different and sinister world, and the contrast made it a hundred times worse.

He couldn't tell his friends, or his family, or his colleagues. And he had his own secret now, as well. His less-than-legitimate meeting with Sophie Townsend yesterday afternoon.

A pointless meeting, to all intents and purposes. If anything, it had confirmed his suspicions, while doing nothing whatsoever to resolve them. *Look, I'm really sorry, but if you want to talk about things like that, you should ask Rachel.* Which, in turn, had created more fears, backed up like rush-hour traffic after a jack-knifed lorry. If something that important *had* happened in Underlyme – and Rachel really cared about him – then wouldn't she have told him about it?

He found himself looking back at their decision to move in together. The casual *why not?* attitude he'd taken suddenly appalled him. He wished he could go back in time, give the implications a little more thought . . .

He thought about Sophie. He'd liked her a lot. Strangely, it hadn't really occurred to him at the time – too much else had been going on, too much awkwardness, embarrassment, self-consciousness. But looking back, he realised there had been something immensely pleasant about her, an unplaceable wholesome sweetness that lingered in his mind like a piece of music.

I'd like to see her again. The thought rose on its own; he struggled to submerge it. He lay sleepless for some time, trying to pretend it wasn't there, telling himself he hadn't already come to a decision.

4

Less than three weeks to go before the Fiat pitch now. Every morning when Rachel opened the appointments calendar in her computer, the date screamed out at her in bold – **Friday, 25th July**, coming closer as she watched.

'Morning,' said Craig, coming into Rachel's office with Neil. 'Sorry we're a bit late.'

They smiled round at Rachel, Sara and Christina as they shut the door and took a seat. 'So,' said Rachel, 'what have you got for us?'

Neil unfolded a sheaf of papers from his sketch-pad. 'Quite a bit,' he said breezily. 'We've been having a good time working on these – reckon you're going to like what we've come up with.'

Rachel was desperately hoping they hadn't taken the wrong direction. They weren't exactly behind schedule, but certainly couldn't afford any more delays. She watched Neil continue with a sense of trepidation. 'We were thinking, there might be a good way to use humour without going over the top,' he was saying, 'and linking it in with some of the key messages. So, as you see, we decided on these.'

Black marker sketches on A3 paper were dealt across the floor, accompanied by a steady running commentary. 'In this one,' Craig announced, 'what we're trying to get across is . . .' Rachel felt the slow dawn of relief, and looked at Sara and Christina out of the corner of her eye. What she saw delighted her; they looked as enthusiastic about these concepts as she felt. 'Well,' she said at last, 'I think they're great. What do you two think?'

Immediate agreement from Sara and Christina prompted a brief conference regarding which of the five campaigns should be extended and finished up for the pitch. Again, they were all in agreement. 'That's great,' Rachel repeated, then, 'Well, looks like we're right on schedule. I suppose the next step has to be getting the media costings from Heather. Have you heard back from her yet, Sara?'

Sara looked blank. 'Don't ask me. I haven't had anything to do with that.'

'I did ask you. On the e-mail I sent you last Monday.' Silence fell like a lead weight; Craig and Neil shifted uncomfortably in their seats, exchanging glances. 'Last Monday morning,' said Rachel. 'You must remember.'

'I didn't get anything from you on Monday morning.' Sara's expression was wary, watchful, defensive. 'I'm sure of it.'

The words stopped just short of direct accusation. Rachel spoke sharply. 'I'll find it. It'll be in my out box – thank God I hardly ever delete things.'

She turned to her computer, moving the mouse as if for dear life. Freezing cold horror drifted over her as she saw she hadn't sent it after all. It was still in her draft e-mails, saved unread, inexplicably unnoticed. 'Christ,' she said. 'Oh, Jesus Christ.'

Craig and Neil got up and left with discreet speed, the door closing quietly behind them. Rachel barely noticed. 'I don't believe this,' she said, mostly to herself. 'I thought you'd read it.'

'Look, Rachel, it's not exactly Sara's fault.' On the surface, Christina's voice was hesitant, but there was a strong undertow of self-righteousness. 'She wasn't to know, was she?'

'You never mentioned it all last week,' Sara chimed in. 'And we're only pushed for time because we waited for Craig and Neil to be free.'

Your decision, your fault – everything about the two of them said it loud and clear. They sat side-by-side, radiating solidarity and judgement in equal measure. Rachel looked at them, and saw a jury looking back. 'Well,' she said at last, and was appalled to hear her voice tremble slightly, 'we'll just have to deal with it the best we can. I'll let Heather know what's happened, see if she can speed things up.'

'It's going to put us *way* behind.' Christina spoke in tones of chilly, clipped authority, antagonism barely veiled. 'We can't draw up the media schedule till we've got the costings.'

Sara nodded. 'It's going to take Heather a *week*.'

'Yes, I know that. There's nothing we can do about it.' Rachel fought for composure, but the ragged edge was unmissable. Beneath the surface of her desk, the remnants of her nails savaged her palms. 'I'll call Heather now. You two can go.'

Sara and Christina left, distrustful glances flickering in Rachel's direction. The door closed with a sharp little click, leaving Rachel alone. Faint murmurs of air-conditioning and striplights had become the only sounds in the world.

She sat as she was, unmoving, for several minutes. Then she called Heather and explained the situation as best she could. Heather said she couldn't promise anything, but she'd do her best to have the costings ready for Monday. Rachel thanked her very much, and hung up.

In the silence of her office, remembered voices echoed. *I'm so proud of you, Rachel*, Nina murmured, and Kate said, *I didn't know you had a cousin working here.* A ghostly hint of Diane's Queen Vic tones: *I knew it wouldn't faze you, Rach. Senior account managers can't afford to get scared of responsibility.*

It was almost a relief to distract herself with the thought of Peter, and the prospect of meeting him for a drink tonight.

5

It wasn't that Sophie kept thinking about Andrew. Most of the time, he was the last thing on her mind. But at odd moments, his image would return, surprising her in the middle of a coffee or a conversation. *No, really*, he'd said, *it's my fault, I shouldn't have asked.* She'd liked him a lot, she realised; someone she could genuinely talk to, as few men had been since her thirteenth summer—

But of course, she couldn't have talked to him about that. Even if they'd known each other well, reached a level of friendship where it was perfectly acceptable to pour your heart out. Whether he'd known it or not, Rachel had defined their conversation in All Bar One, established its unbreakable boundaries, the certain knowledge that she'd be furious if she could see them together.

Never mind if she could see them talking about *those* things—

No point going over that meeting in her mind. It had been awkward, and then nice, and then over. Rising from her desk, Sophie headed towards the kitchen and the water-cooler. Even with the air-conditioning on, it was too hot, and the afternoon was maddening through the windows – redolent of Pimms and Wimbledon, long lazy days and nothing to do but sunbathe. Across the office, she could see Jessie on the phone.

The kitchen was shadowy and colder. Sophie topped up a plastic cup, and her gaze strayed to the crowded notice-board. At first, she saw nothing much of interest, then noticed something new. INTERNAL VACANCY, she read, ACCOUNT ADMINISTRATOR.

Suddenly interested, she skimmed it, seeing it involved much the same sort of thing as her current job, only based on the account handling floor. *Strong admin skills, high level of organisation,* she read, then, *This is an ideal opportunity to progress to the role of Junior Account Manager. Please check with your line manager before applying.*

Back at her desk, the notice lingered in her thoughts. It became more and more attractive as she thought about it. Comfortable where she was now, she'd written off the daydreams she'd had on the train to Waterloo – a silly small-town fantasy of future achievement, designed to distract her from terror – but the notice brought them back. She didn't want to spend her whole life like this, after all. Surely she was capable of more than filing.

I'll ask Lisa about it first thing on Monday, Sophie thought, *as soon as she gets back from holiday,* and at that moment, the phone rang on her desk.

'It's me, Andrew.' This time, she recognised the male voice at once. 'How's it going?'

'Oh – I'm all right.' Her bewilderment was absolute, and she spoke with the automatic reflex of catching a ball, throwing it back. 'How are you?'

'Not so bad.' A pregnant silence. When he spoke again, the slick veneer of small talk was gone, replaced by awkwardness. 'Look, I was just wondering if you'd like to meet up sometime. For a drink or something. For a chat.'

She looked across the busy open-plan office, saw nobody paying attention to her side of the exchange. Still she lowered her voice. 'You know I won't tell you anything about Rachel,' she said. 'I can't.'

'I know,' he said. 'I don't want you to.'

6

At six thirty, Rachel checked her watch. Time to leave. The office beyond the glass partition had drained empty some time ago, leaving a forest of desks and black computer screens, a scene of desolation. Something cold ran up the back of her neck.

Outside, the rosy-gold evening reminded her of too much. It whispered in her mind like a false and gloating friend, as she headed towards a place she wasn't supposed to be, murmuring of high summer in Acacia Avenue, Aunt Linda and Uncle Brian, of secrets and betrayals and the worst thing of all—

You're lying!

—then she was reaching the parked MG, driving fast and erratically towards the unknown.

In next to no time, she was there, at the anonymous-looking pub called the Turk's Head, stepping into a quiet world of dark wood and faded red velvet, a handful of muted two-way conversations. An unattended fruit machine fizzed and muttered by the bar; behind it, a bored-looking young man in shirtsleeves stood, idly polishing glasses. Rachel walked past, towards the back tables where Peter sat.

'Rachel.' He rose from his seat. 'What do you want to drink?'

'I'll have a pineapple juice, please.'

She watched him walk over to the bar, and return with her drink. 'Thanks,' she said. 'I can't stay long, I'm afraid.'

'I don't mind. I just wanted to see you.'

The longing in his voice was naked. She looked at him for a long second, suddenly curious. 'Why me?' she asked at last. 'Why not some other girl?'

'Because she wouldn't be you.' He turned his head unexpectedly. 'Look at them,' he said quietly.

Rachel looked in the direction that he indicated. A group of young women had just come in, noisy and ebullient, shrieking and giggling their way over to the bar. 'What about them?'

'They're all the same. And they don't even know it.' His voice betrayed a detached contempt; indefinable emotion flickered in his eyes. 'They think they know what life's about. They don't know a thing.'

Andrew's image rose abruptly in her mind. She forced it back like bile, struggling to imitate Diane's bright, chilly voice, Diane's arch, professional little smile. 'Do you? Know what life's about?'

'Yes,' he said. 'And you do, too.'

'What's it about?'

'Being alone.'

She looked at him, and saw far too much of herself looking back. 'That's not true,' she said. 'It's easy to be part of things.'

He watched her, half smiling. 'You don't believe that.'

'How do you know?'

'I just do. I can see it in your eyes,' he said. 'Other people don't see that. They don't notice a thing.'

It was exactly what she'd thought about him, as she'd watched him in the office. She looked at him across the cigarette-scarred table: the bony, almost-beautiful face, the disturbing, unblinking eyes of the obsessive. A sense of kinship suddenly appalled her. 'That's not true,' she said quickly. 'You're wrong.' She finished her pineapple juice in one long gulp. 'I'm sorry,' she said, 'I've got to go. I'll be late home. I'll see you at work.' Then she was turning, hurrying to escape, feeling his eyes on her back.

7

She was perfect.

He came out of the tube station at Tooting Broadway, and started walking. It was almost full dark now, the quiet streets stirring with intermittent life. Bright light from the fish-and-chip shop, the kebab shop, the Chinese takeaway. Crowded cameos in pub windows; the people who understood nothing.

She understood. Even though she'd denied it. He hadn't needed to talk to her to know how deeply she shared his isolation – he could *hear* her, *feel* her pinging in his head like sonar. He needed to know nothing about her but that single fact. They were mirrors to each other; they were the same.

That was love. You knew love when you found it, however incongruous the context – a glossy office crowded with pot-plants and ringing telephones, a shabby council flat, rank with Grandad's Woodbines—

Mind, you're not to tell anyone, Pete boy, the old man whispered in his mind. *It ain't safe. Put you in jail for things like that, they do.*

The last few streets unwound under the pallid streetlamps, leading to the tall, shabby Victorian semi with the broken gate. He let himself in. One of the other residents was talking on the hall payphone. 'See you on Saturday night,' he was saying. 'I'll bring some booze round, and . . .'

A perfunctory nod to the man on the phone, and Peter was walking past, ascending the stairs. On the landing, the door to one bedsit was ajar, and he could hear female voices inside, shrieking laughter. His gaze fixed on the brightly lit gap for a long second – always noisy, always crowded, an unofficial house common-room he never went into.

But that didn't matter now. He had Rachel to think about – her and Grandad's secret. That was one of the reasons why he'd moved out of his mother's house as soon as he could afford to. It had never seemed quite safe in his bedroom there, well hidden as it had been. He unlocked the door to the shabby pin-neatness of his bedsit, and locked it again behind him before turning towards the forbidden.

He thought he might go for a walk that night.

8

Half eleven on Monday morning. Rachel was sitting at her desk when the knock came.

'Come in.'

It was Diane. 'Morning, Rach,' she said chummily. 'Not interrupting anything, am I?'

'Not at all.' She watched Diane closely, alert to danger. 'What can I do for you?'

'Just felt like a chat, really. Been a while since we caught up.' Diane sat down, crossing her ankles. 'So how's the senior account manager life been treating you?'

'Well, can't complain,' said Rachel, smiling. 'It's all going very well.'

'Good.' The silence lasted a beat too long before Diane spoke again, casually. 'By the way, how's the Fiat pitch going? Been meaning to ask for a while.'

So that was what this was really about. In Diane's words, she sensed the presence of Sara and Christina, and held on to her smile with every reserve of strength she possessed. 'It's going well,' she heard herself repeating. 'I must say, I'm pretty confident.'

'Well, that's terrific.' Diane's smile was dazzling, but the water-coloured eyes were as chilly and observant as ever. 'Heard something about the media costings running late, but I knew someone must have got their wires crossed. You'd never make a cock-up like that – you have got them, haven't you?'

Rachel had never been more aware of her own heartbeat. She envisioned Diane's arch, approving smile shattering on the floor in a split second. 'I'll have them first thing tomorrow. Heather said she'd e-mail them through tonight.'

'I *knew* they must be on their way. If I didn't trust you with my life, Rach, I'd never have fought like I did to get you here.' Diane's gaze swept the stylish office – a benevolent aunt, a fairy godmother. 'Reckon you're going to walk this, you know.'

As the door closed behind Diane, Rachel looked through the glass panel, and saw Sara and Christina paying a little too much attention to her exit. Then she saw them glance at each other, a fleeting look that instantly confirmed her suspicions. One or both of them had had a quiet word with Diane, almost certainly no more than a discreet hint; they'd know perfectly well that a direct accusation of incompetence would antagon- ise Diane at once. Saying just enough to extricate themselves swiftly from the wreckage, in the event of disaster. *We were worried all along,* they'd say. *Even spoke to Diane about it – but there was nothing we could do.*

The words she'd spoken just now played back in her mind. *I'll have them first thing tomorrow.* One phone call to Heather could tell Diane a different story – but Rachel was pretty sure she'd never make that call. She found her finger in her mouth again, teeth gnawing, gnawing.

I'm just buying extra time. Diane's going to find out whatever I do – I'm backing into a corner. Checking her watch, she saw that her hand was shaking badly. It was approaching twelve noon. She picked up her handbag and walked quickly out of the office. Suddenly, she didn't want to see Peter at all. In her mind, he'd begun to feel like a high, unshielded ledge; the world around her like hands pushing her towards it.

9

At lunchtime, Sophie and Jessie left the building together. 'Guess what?' Sophie asked, as they stepped out. 'I asked Lisa if I could apply for that Account Admin job, and she said she'd even give me a reference. She thinks I'm in with a really good chance.'

'That's fantastic,' said Jessie. 'Mind you, I'm not surprised. You've been working so hard. You'd make a hell of an account manager, one day.'

'I wish.' Sophie spoke wistfully. 'It would be great.'

'You're just after the free sandwiches, aren't you?' demanded Jessie, and they laughed, joining the sandwich-shop queue.

There was a maddening, uncomfortable itch at the back of Sophie's mind. As they came out, she couldn't prevent herself from speaking. 'You know, I'm sort of worried about a friend of mine. She's meeting this guy tonight, and I think she might be making a mistake.'

Jessie looked at her curiously. 'How come?'

'He's already going out with someone. Someone she knows.'

'A friend of hers?'

'Not really. Not any more.' Sophie took a deep breath. 'They were friends when they were kids, but that was a long time ago. They hardly see each other these days.'

'What's he like?' Jessie asked. 'The guy?'

'My friend says he seems really nice. But you know, she's not sure. For all she knows, he might just be looking for a one-night stand.'

Jessie grinned. 'Would she be up for that?'

'God, no.' Sophie spoke too vehemently, and hurried back to a tone of disinterested concern. 'She hasn't got much experience with men. She's had a few boyfriends, but, you know, nothing serious – I think she just went out with them because you *have* to have boyfriends, people think you're weird otherwise. She never really talked to them properly, she never understood them.' They strolled on, side by side. 'I suppose she's led a bit of a sheltered life.'

'It sounds like she's taking a risk.' Sophie's heart plummeted, and she struggled not to show her dismay before Jessie spoke again. 'But still, I reckon she should go for it. Nothing ventured, nothing gained. It's not like he's married or anything.'

'No,' Sophie said quickly, 'he's not.'

Back in the office, she tried to concentrate, but found it impossible to distract her mind from Andrew. Fears and hopes and doubts swarmed through her thoughts, buzzing furiously. Jessie was right, she told herself, even though she'd had to hide behind an alias for fear of Jessie's disapproval. There was nothing to lose, she was doing nothing truly wrong in meeting Rachel's boyfriend for a drink. Already, a part of her had entered the bar, was anxiously watching the door for his arrival.

10

Rachel was driving home. They still didn't have the media costings. Heather had said she'd deliver them in a few days' time. Sara and Christina's silent condemnation had become blatant.

A car was coming out of a side street, ahead of her. Rachel was about to hammer straight past, then realised it wasn't stopping. She slammed on the brakes at the last second, an ace away from collision. Horns blared furiously as she sat stock still for an endless moment. *Christ*, she thought, *I hate driving when I feel like this.* She forced herself to set off again, anxiety pounding at her temples.

Andrew would be out that night, at his weekly poker game. Part of her was relieved that she wouldn't have to feign happiness when she got in, pretend that everything was all right. Still, the idea of the silent flat ahead unnerved her. Remembering that they needed to stock up on some groceries, she headed for the all-night garage shop.

Inside, she got a basket, and ticked items off a mental list – washing-up liquid, black pepper, bin bags, milk. She was approaching the till when déjà vu hit her out of nowhere, the rest of the shop blurring, the drinks section leaping out in ultra-sharp focus. Endless rows of bottles on shelves, glinting in the light.

She walked towards it as if hypnotised, a terrified passenger in her own body, screaming frantic warnings at herself. *Stop. Stop.* And still she walked, remembering the taste of oblivion from all those years ago – the relief of laying down the lead weight of tension, of finding a secret freedom from fear. Of temporarily forgetting –

A sunny garden. A dark bedroom. Nina's mounting concern and bewilderment, terrible beyond expression, juxtaposed with a secret that could never be confessed – finding an escape from it all in the very thing she dreaded most. The voluntary surrender of control, the bottle passing from hand to hand in the promenade shelter –

You finished with that yet, Rach? she remembered, and she watched her hand as if it belonged to someone else, lifting a half-bottle of vodka off the shelf, putting it in the basket with her other purchases.

Behind the wheel, she drove erratically. The carrier bag was under the passenger seat. The bottle inside it screamed out at her all the way home, promising a night of freedom and forgetfulness. In her mouth, she tasted terror.

11

The time was almost half seven, and Fusion was getting busy. Standing by the bar, Andrew sipped at his pint, keeping a close eye on the main doors through shifting crowds of people.

You're stupid to be meeting her here, he thought starkly. *Why not somewhere further away?* Guilt, perhaps, an attempt to pretend to himself that this was all above board. As long as they met this close to Rachel's office, he couldn't be doing anything furtive or secret. If Rachel saw them, he could say *hi, Rach, we just ran into each other, and—*

But there was something deeper there, too. A part of him – mostly unrecognised – would *like* to be seen. He couldn't bring himself to precipitate a blazing argument with Rachel; domestic pacifism was a religion drilled into him from his earliest days. But to have events beyond his control do it for him was quite another matter – to have *them* inspire confrontation, possible break-up . . .

You're hoping for too much, an inner voice told him flatly. This relationship won't just wander off on its own, Andrew. In case you haven't noticed, Rachel's living with you now. You've only got two options. Stay with her, or tell her straight out that—

A glimpse of dark-blonde hair through the pressing crowd, and Sophie was approaching. With a combination of effort and relief, he pressed the mute button on his thoughts.

'Hi,' he said, as she reached him. 'What would you like to drink?'

'Oh, thanks very much. A white wine spritzer, please.'

This time, the barman served them quickly. There was only one table free, by a window. They sat down across from each other.

'So how's adland been treating you?' he asked.

'Oh, not so bad.' At first she spoke casually, then confidentially. 'Well, good, I suppose. I found out I'm in with a chance at this job I really want. I've been thinking about it all day.'

'Good stuff. What sort of job is it?'

'Just admin – pretty much what I'm doing at the moment. But the prospects are miles better.' Something wistful stirred in her voice. 'It's supposed to be a good way in if you want to move up to being a junior account handler. I'd love to do that.'

'I'll keep everything crossed for you,' he said. 'When'll you get the verdict?'

'I'm not sure. I applied this afternoon, and the interviews are next week.'

The conversation moved on, in the noise and music and busyness of office crowds unwinding from the day's pressures. It reminded him of evenings he'd used to have with girls, straightforward conversation, easy laughter. He was very aware of his growing attraction towards her. At first, he hadn't really noticed the way she looked, but now he did. Things about her jumped out at him: the way her hair caught the last of the evening light, the way her eyes opened wide when she smiled. The subtle hint of her body spray as she moved closer towards him. They talked about everything but Rachel, and what they really thought about each other, and the stark fact that they shouldn't be here now.

An eventual lull in the conversation, and Sophie checked her watch. He saw shock in her eyes. 'Oh God, I didn't know it was so late,' she said. 'I'd better get going – I've got to be at work for eight sharp tomorrow.'

'No worries. I'll walk you to the station.'

Farringdon station was five minutes' walk away, and they travelled side by side, deliberately not touching. The air of friendship between them had become too casual, too hearty, unconvincing.

'Well,' she said, as they stopped outside the station, 'it's been good to meet you again. I've had a really nice night.'

'Me too.' An awkward pause, noisy with passers-by. 'Can I give you a call again sometime?'

'I'll give you my mobile number. I might as well.' Her voice was far too offhand, subtly apprehensive. 'Have you got a pen?'

He did, and a crumpled old receipt in his wallet. She read her number out, he wrote it down quickly on the back of the receipt. 'Great,' he said at last, tucking it into his pocket. 'I'll call you later in the week, okay?'

'Okay.' This was the moment to kiss or not to kiss, and they looked at each other knowing it. He was both relieved and intensely disappointed to feel that moment pass. 'Well,' she said, 'I'd better go. Bye, Andrew.'

He stood and watched her walk away, into the stark lights of the station, through the ticket barriers, vanishing round a corner. Half ten on Monday night, and he was alone.

Couldn't go back to Camden yet, not on his poker night. Paradoxically, coming home early might make Rachel suspicious; he didn't know why that should matter, but simultaneously knew that it did. Might as well meet the guys after all – better late than never. He got a ticket from the machine and went through the barriers himself, deliberately not recognising his disappointment as he saw the empty platform.

In Maida Vale, the air of Harry's flat was thick with smoke and noise, ebulliently macho as always, five or six nice professional boyfriends cutting loose for a night of freedom. 'Where the bloody hell have *you* been?' demanded Tim, and Charlie said, 'Get a beer out of the fridge, you'll have to sit this one out.' It was a relief to be on the outskirts of things for an hour or so. He couldn't quite get into the spirit tonight, and his laughter sounded effortful. At last, he was dealt in. 'Thought Rachel must have locked you in,' Harry complained. Andrew smiled, blamed the pressures of work, fell silent. Deep down, he couldn't concentrate on the game's progress, and luck alone stopped him losing more than twenty pounds.

When he finally got back to Camden, it was almost one o'clock. As his key turned in the lock, he realised the extent of his exhaustion. Didn't even have the energy to get himself a hot drink from the kitchen. Quietly, he let himself into the bathroom, and when he'd washed and brushed his teeth, he went even more quietly to bed. In the darkness, Rachel faced away from him. The pressures of their relationship, he noticed, seemed to be affecting him far more than her. She was dead to the world.

He fell asleep thinking about Sophie.

12

Rachel woke up slowly. She felt awful, weak and sick; nausea throbbed inside her. There was something eerie about the light in the room, filtering through the drawn curtains; casting a faint glow across the shadowed dressing table, the shadowed floor. She turned her head to see the clock radio, saw it was almost half six.

Jesus Christ, I have to be up in quarter of an hour. Wondering exactly how much she'd had to drink, she traced last night back in her mind, and was alarmed to find a blank space where memories should have been. She was in her pyjamas, but had no recollection of putting them on. She must have taken her make-up off and brushed her teeth, because she always did, but she couldn't remember doing that either.

The thought yanked her out of her reflective torpor like a sudden smell of burning. She hurried out of bed, through the hallway. In the bathroom, the blinds were drawn, and she snapped the light on. The unforgiving mirror showed dark circles and pallor under harsh white light, and something worse. Black smudges round her eyes, faint after a night's drugged sleep, but still there.

I always take my eye make-up off. The rest of it must have worn off in the night . . .

The idea that she'd crashed out with her make-up on was inexplicably terrifying. She splashed her face over and over, scrubbed with exfoliator, toned, moisturised. She brushed her teeth for a good six minutes, reached for her make-up bag with a shaking hand. A little heavier on the bronzer than usual. Her pallor demanded it. When she'd finished, she looked at herself in the mirror. A stranger stood and looked back at her with cynical, appraising eyes.

The alarm went off in the bedroom. She could hear Andrew getting up, moving into the kitchen, turning the radio on. She followed him in, steeling herself to be business-as-usual.

'Morning,' she said in the doorway.

'Morning.' He was putting some bread in the toaster, looked round and studied her closely. 'You okay? You look a bit under the weather.'

'I'm fine. Maybe a bit tired.' Her head was throbbing as she went to the fridge; she poured herself a long glass of orange juice, longing to gulp, forcing herself to sip as he looked at her. 'I had to stay late last night, and—'

'What's the matter?'

In the pale, fresh morning sunlight, the silence seemed to stretch out for ever. Her gaze had zoomed in on the kitchen counter, directly behind his left shoulder. The half-bottle of vodka, entirely empty, stood by the sink. She dragged her eyes back to him, her voice too high, too quick.

'Nothing. Just remembered something I've got to get done at work today. It slipped my mind for a bit. You know how it is.' Her mouth moved as on autopilot. The bottle shrieked out from the edge of her vision. 'So how was the game last night? Have a nice time?'

'Not bad,' he said, then, with some concern, 'You *sure* you're all right?'

'I'm fine. Just fine.' She looked back at him, smiling her terror in the sunlight, desperately willing him not to turn his head to the right. 'Was that the paper?'

'I didn't hear anything.'

'It sounded like the paper. Being delivered.'

He eyed her uncertainly. 'Well – I'll go and have a look.'

As soon as he'd left the kitchen, Rachel grabbed the bottle and shoved it deep into the bin, sliming her hands to the wrists. Her heart was hammering. She went to the sink, scrubbed her hands as if her life depended on it, and was drying them on a tea towel as he came back in. 'No,' he said, 'nothing.'

'Must have been hearing things. Tinnitus, maybe.' The force of her relief was extraordinary – she was almost hysterical with it, laughing a cocktail-party laugh at nothing. She saw him looking at her strangely. 'I'd better get a move on anyway,' she said. 'I'll be late.'

She showered, styled her hair, and changed into a neat trouser-suit. When she returned to the kitchen, the paper had arrived, and he was reading it at the table. 'Well,' she said, 'I'm off. I'll take the rubbish out – might as well.'

'It's okay. I'll do it.'

'No, really. It's fine. I'll see you later.'

Outside, at the communal wheelie-bins behind the building, she hoisted the tied black bin-bag inside, heard it drop, a faint tell-tale shatter of glass. She didn't know whether Andrew would have noticed it or not. The fact that he *might* have done was enough, the idea that he *might* have seen it by the sink. And relief ebbed away far too quickly, leaving only what it had washed up on the shore – strange things she didn't want to look at too closely, drowned, rotted.

She drove. The DJ chattered on from the radio. 'And it's gonna be a scorcher,' he was enthusing. 'Weathermen say we're set for the biggest heatwave in more than ten years; yes, listeners, it's summer in the city . . .' Amber changed to red ahead. Rachel screeched to a halt. In the rear-view mirror, a glimpse of her own face appalled her: a death's head over a Jigsaw shirt, terror shrieking from its eyes.

Up the curving white-stone steps, through the gleaming sun-drenched vastness of reception. Rachel walked, barely taking in a thing. She waited for a lift with a handful of others, got out at the third floor alone. An image of her face in the rear-view mirror led her straight to the Ladies', the mirrors by the washbasins, the make-up in her bag.

Inside, the Ladies' was deserted. She applied more make-up with a kind of paranoiac attention to detail; her lipliner was slightly smudged, she saw. She wiped it off, sharpened the liner pencil, drew it a second time. It still looked lopsided. She wiped it off again, drew it again. The longer she looked at her reflection, the more she saw wrong, and trapped, yammering panic took hold of her; she put on more foundation and bronzer and mascara, but nothing seemed to make any difference. When she looked at her watch, she realised she'd been here almost ten minutes. With an immense effort, she put her make-up back in her handbag, turned away from the mirrors. She found it disturbingly easy to imagine herself still standing here in an hour's time.

She was hoping to make the journey into her own office unobserved, but as she walked into the main open-plan space, a familiar voice rang out to her right. 'Hi, Rach.' Nothing else for it – she walked over to Kate's desk, smiling. 'How's it going?' Kate continued. 'Haven't seen you in ages.'

'Oh, I'm fine. Just been tied up on that Fiat pitch – still am, really.'

'How's that going?'

Her headache buzzed behind her eyes like an enraged bluebottle hellbent on escape. She could find nothing in her mind but lethargic stock responses. 'Fine,' she said, 'it's going fine.'

'That's good.' Kate studied her for a second. 'You look a bit knackered this morning, Rach. Suppose you got in late last night.'

Rachel looked back blankly. 'How do you mean?'

'You went out with your cousin and Andrew, didn't you? I saw them in Fusion on the way home last night – expect you were at the bar. I'd have popped in and said hi, if I hadn't been in such a hurry.'

The printer hummed to itself across the big sunny office. There was no other sound. 'What time was that?' Rachel asked slowly. 'When you saw us?'

'Must have been about seven thirty, eight-ish.' Kate spoke amiably. 'I didn't get out of here till really late. Can't believe the bloody hours I'm putting in lately.'

'Too much to do, too little time.' Rachel heard her own voice coming from a long way away. 'Speaking of which, I'd better get on.'

'Yeah. See you later, Rach. We should go for lunch some time.'

Rachel barely heard her as she went into her own office, closing the door behind her. The words she'd just heard played over and over, louder and louder in her head. *I saw them in Fusion on the way home last night*, Kate had said blithely, and looking at the photograph by the computer, Rachel saw the worst thing in the world: the smiling man with his arm round her shoulder turning into a stranger as she watched.

14

Ten past eleven, and Peter was taking out last month's magazines from the little side lounge in the creative department, replacing them with the latest copies. The creative department was almost entirely male, and its choice of reading matter tended to reflect that; a glossy, suntanned blonde pouted up at Peter from the cover of the topmost magazine, Wonderbra cleavage spilling out from unbuttoned white shirt, behind loosened school tie. As he took the old copies down to the basement, a wave of loathing overcame him. He remembered the other boys back at school, what they'd seemed to think of as *sex appeal.*

Not that he'd ever cared what they thought. They'd probably been able to feel that indifference, even if they hadn't understood it. In the early years of school, he'd sensed the puzzlement behind insults that meant nothing to him. In later years, the insults had ended abruptly, and he'd found himself treated with watchful arm's-length caution. He hadn't cared about that, either. By then, he'd had something real to think about.

They put you in jail for things like that, Grandad had said, and at last he'd had something he could love. *You're not to tell anyone I let you see it, Pete boy—*

He hadn't. Of course he hadn't. Nobody knew it existed even now, now Grandad was dead and it was his.

At twelve noon, he made his lunchtime rounds quickly on the account handlers' floor, and came to the only door that mattered. He heard her voice from inside, sweet as a reprieve. 'Come in.'

He did. Closing the door behind him, he saw her as if for the first time; something pure and perfect, sealed away from the world's corruption. In her, he saw both himself and an idealised other. 'Hi, Rachel,' he said. 'What do you want from Pret?'

'I think I'll have the sushi again.' Sunlight poured through the window behind her. He watched her become luminous. 'It's a lovely day, isn't it? It's going to be the hottest summer in years, they say.'

It was the only thing he disliked about her, this sporadic nervous chatter – there was no need for conversation between them, she must know that, as he did. Silence was only uncomfortable to people who understood nothing. He jotted, looked at her again, forgiving instantly.

'Listen,' he said, 'do you want to go out for a drink again?'

'I don't know.' He saw her gaze flicker to the photograph he hated the sight of, before she spoke again, voice odd and ragged in repetition. '*I don't know.*'

Silence. He didn't know if she expected him to entreat, but he didn't entreat. She would agree. He was sure of it.

'I can't stay long,' she said at last. 'You know that.'

'It doesn't matter.' It was true – he wanted nothing more from her than her brief presence. Just to see her was enough. 'What about seven thirty next Tuesday night? At the Turk's Head?'

'Make it nine thirty,' she said. 'I might have to stay late.'

'All right,' he said. 'I'll see you there.'

Out of reception, he walked towards Pret, moving through crowded streets that seemed increasingly hateful to him, seeing too much that he longed to destroy. But he wasn't alone any more. His goddess walked with him in his mind. He knew she always would.

15

Rachel left on time because there was no need to stay late. In the very near future, she was well aware it would be a different story. As soon as Heather e-mailed the media costings through, she'd be working all the hours God sent.

She drove, wondering why the hell she'd agreed to meet Peter again. But deep down, she knew. Partly that compulsion she had no control over. Still, for once, there was more to it than that. She would have turned to anything to escape this new and unthinkable fear, any diversion, any escape.

You went out with your cousin and Andrew, didn't you? Kate's voice whispered in her ear. *I saw them in Fusion on the way home last night.*

Again, when she got back just before six, Andrew wasn't home. More than ever, she felt the weight of helplessness, and longed to ask him what he'd really done last night, knowing it was unthinkable. An innocent, chance meeting would have been referred to in the morning, and he'd mentioned nothing.

Maybe Kate was wrong. Maybe it was someone who just looked like Andrew – she couldn't have seen that clearly looking through a wine-bar window, looking at a crowd. You know what Kate's like, she never checks her facts ...

She was walking through the hallway, trying to soothe the defensive babble of thoughts, when her gaze was caught by something on the floor. Andrew had left his leather jacket behind, she saw. It had fallen off its hook. In her mind's eye, she could see him clearly, coming in in the small hours of the morning, absently shrugging it off.

She picked it up, was halfway to putting it back on the hook when an impulse took hold of her. She held it in one hand and burrowed into the pockets with the other. She'd feared and expected a Fusion receipt, but the only receipt she brought out said *Enrico's Lunches*. She was about to replace it when she saw something had been written on the back, and turned it over.

A mobile phone number. In Andrew's writing.

It could be anyone's, she told herself savagely. *It could have been there days, weeks* – but before she knew what she was doing or had made any conscious decision, she was at the hallway telephone, picking up the receiver, dialling the number on the back of the receipt. The ringing tone began in an unknown world. Suddenly, she was very aware of her surroundings; a golden edge to the light hinted at imminent sunset.

'Hello?'

A young, male voice, a voice she'd never heard before in her life. Relief crashed down on her. 'I'm sorry,' she said. 'I think I've got the wrong number.'

'Oh, it's not my mobile. She's just gone to the kitchen.' The voice turned away slightly, called. 'Sophie – call for you!'

Rachel hung up.

Book Four

It happened last night.

Of course, I knew it would. I've been avoiding being alone with him for ages. At first, I wasn't quite sure why, just something about the way he looked at me. Then he started touching me, and I knew for sure. Why else did I tell her, if I hadn't known for sure that when they were gone he was going to—

But it doesn't feel like something I've been expecting. It feels like something that just jumped out at me.

They left yesterday. The taxi came at half nine in the morning. It was all busy and crowded and smiley, the grown-ups getting cases out of the hallway – you know where this is, you know where that is. I didn't even look at her. She didn't look at me, either. There was something weird about it in all that chatter. Like not talking to someone at their birthday party.

Her mum noticed. I could see she noticed. Kept wondering if she'd say anything about it in the taxi or on the train or when they were unpacking. Ask if we'd had an argument or something, and then I imagined her bursting out crying and telling her mum what I'd told her, and I imagined her mum putting her hand over her own mouth like I've never seen anyone do in real life. The way you act horror in a school play. We've got to go back right now, *I imagined her mum saying.* Why didn't you tell me, you stupid girl?

But of course, her mum wouldn't ask about kids' stuff. And she wouldn't tell the truth even if her mum did ask. Anyway, it's too late now. After last night, it's never going to be the same.

I stood next to him and watched the taxi drive off. He

133

waved at them. I didn't. When the taxi had gone, we went back into the house and didn't say anything. The phone went in the hallway and he went to get it. I went out into the garden and swung on the swing with a book she'd left behind. It felt like wearing her clothes, pretending to be her. Pretending to be safe.

So hot, it was. I could hear crickets. It seemed all wrong to be scared on a day like that. I should have been thinking about lemonade and daydreams, but I could feel him inside the house, knew I'd have to go in sooner or later.

Normally, afternoons last years in the holidays. That one didn't. It seemed like no time before he was standing at the back door, calling me in for tea. I looked at my watch, and it was almost seven o'clock. They were having a barbecue next door. I could smell it. When I got off the swing, I could hear them talking – a woman saying something about Florida, some little kids running round the garden shrieking. Through the fence, I could see one of them squirting a water pistol.

It's weird. In the nightmares I had before, the bad things always happened in dark forests and underground tunnels, with nobody there to see what happened. But this felt worse.

Nothing happened in the kitchen. We just had tea. He read the paper and I read her book. When I'd finished eating, he said to leave the washing-up, he'd do it. I went upstairs. The bedroom felt strange, looked different. I tried to tell myself maybe I was wrong, maybe she'd been right after all. Maybe I'd been imagining things.

I didn't see him for the rest of the evening. Could hear him moving about downstairs, but that was all. When it got to nine thirty, I washed my face, brushed my teeth and went to bed. At first, I thought I couldn't get to sleep knowing he was there. But I did. I could hear the crickets from the garden. I just drifted off.

What woke me up was the bedroom door opening. Just a slow, creaky little sound, but it snapped me wide awake. I sat up. The light was on in the hallway. He was standing in the door like one of the silhouettes we did in art last year, a shape cut out of black card.

It's all right, he said. Don't be frightened.

He came into the room. Stopped being a silhouette and started being part of the dark. It surprised me how nothing I felt, in a distant sort of way. Like I was standing on the other side of the room and watching it happen. And when he sat down on the bed and put his hand under the duvet, my mind was just blank. Just heard things. Rustling. His breathing. The scratchy metal sound of his zipper—

But I don't want to think about that. Not now. I'm writing this behind the shed because it's safe here, and it's cool here, and I don't want to think about that. Don't want to think it's going to happen again tonight. Next door's kids are chasing each other round the garden again. Their mum's calling them in for lunch. He'll call me in soon. It's nearly one o'clock.

If this was a book or a movie, I'd run away. But I know I'm not going to. There's nowhere to go, for one thing. People would only catch me and bring me back here. And I wouldn't be able to tell them either, just like I can't tell the grown-ups next door. Even if they're nice, they wouldn't believe me, wouldn't understand.

I don't blame them for that. But I blame her. She's my friend, she's my cousin, she knows him – she should have understood. And she didn't. Just went away. Keep imagining her off with her mum and wondering what they're up to – wonder if she's remembering what I said, what she said.

I don't think so. I think she's forgotten all about me. I hate her worse than I hate him. I hate her worse than anyone in the world.

The way I feel today, I think I could kill her.

1

Before the arrival of the media costings, the days at work had dragged. Now they raced. Rachel chased after lost time, saw it as a tiny speck on the horizon – it grew no nearer as she ran, would vanish if she paused for breath.

July 25th. The date screamed at her from her calendar. Small landmarks took on appalling significance: the Wimbledon finals, a major new film release, anything with an established place in time. The last of the scenery, unwinding towards a place of execution.

Each morning brought tense, rushed meetings with Sara and Christina. 'I don't think the Powerpoint presentation's going to be ready on time,' Sara said, and Christina added, 'We'll just have to do the best we can now.' Two pairs of accusing eyes, two cold, identical stares. Alone in her office, Rachel closed her eyes and saw them talking about her – their hushed and furious voices in the kitchen appallingly clear in her mind.

July 25th. She froze at the date like a rabbit in headlights. In bed at night she couldn't sleep, she'd feel one foot tapping rhythmically against the other, marking out the seconds as if she needed to keep count. They slipped away fast. *July 25th,* and there was so much more to do, so much further to run, and she stayed in the office till nine or ten every night, accomplishing nowhere near enough. A small dent in a mountain of backed-up work, like trying to empty a pond with a jug. On Tuesday evening, she couldn't leave the office to meet Peter as they'd arranged. When she saw him the next day, she told him why she hadn't been able to make it, and they rescheduled their Turk's Head evening for a later date.

July 25th, and then it was the 15th, and the 16th, and the 17th, and Friday was ending, and the pitch was less than a week away.

And constantly, the steady, throbbing background noise of Andrew and Sophie. Two names that had no business in the same sentence, their juxtaposition nightmarish. Longing to ask Andrew what was going on, not daring. Their life together had taken on the character of an uneasy flatshare; she came in at night and he'd already eaten, she'd had a sandwich or a bagel at her desk. Each night, they exchanged nothing but brief asides: *the bathroom's free, good night.* Another postcard came from Helen. He didn't mention it. She saw it in the hallway one morning, on her way to the car park.

July 25th, and she'd never wanted a drink as badly as she did now, a kind of physical hunger for oblivion, as impossible to ignore as starvation. Impossible to give in to when Andrew was there. The idea of him seeing her drunk appalled her. A long, quiet weekend stretched out like torture.

On Sunday, when Andrew was out playing squash, Nina rang. Her voice seemed to come from very far away. She asked how Rachel was, and Rachel told her she was fine, that everything was fine, and Nina sent her love to Andrew. And when Rachel hung up, she realised her forehead was cold and slick with sweat.

July 25th, and then it was Monday morning.

2

At half ten on Monday morning, the phone went on Sophie's desk. She picked it up on the third ring.

'Hi, Sophie? It's me.'

Relief hit her hard – despite herself, she'd begun to think Andrew had forgotten her.

'How's it going?' he continued. 'Have a good weekend?'

'Fine, thanks.' She lowered her voice slightly. 'Spent most of it thinking about that job, to be honest. I've got my interview for it at half eleven today.'

'Well, I'll say a prayer for you. Not that you'll need it.' This time, the pause had a pregnant quality, heralding a question. 'Fancy meeting up again?'

He was doing that voice again, that far-too-casual oh-why-not voice. She recognised it, but when she spoke, she found herself doing the same. 'That would be nice. I'd like that.'

'How about tomorrow night?'

She hadn't been expecting to meet him again so soon – but there was nothing to stop her agreeing. 'Tomorrow night's fine.'

'Great. Say Fusion again, half seven?' She murmured assent, and they said their goodbyes.

Sophie hung up, smiling slightly, before stark reality flooded in like ice-cold water. However normal and comfortable it felt to talk with Andrew, he was still forbidden territory. Looking back, she saw innocent conversation become shadowed and dangerous with betrayal – Rachel's man and Rachel's cousin, edging uncertainly round mutual attaction.

But this wasn't the time to think about that. Her interview on the third floor was less than half an hour away now. She sat and tried to work, minutes ticking away in her head. Lisa came out of her office, and stopped off by Sophie's desk. 'Good luck, Sophie,' she said. 'I think you're in with a very good chance,' and then she was walking away.

Sophie forced herself to block Andrew out of her mind, along with Rachel. Nothing mattered but the job on the account handling floor now, the stepping-stone to the better things she'd hoped for. The clock across the room said it was eleven fifteen. Time to go.

On the third floor, she walked quickly through a vast, crowded office, dotted here and there with pot-plants. She feared a chance sighting of Rachel, but she couldn't see her at any of the desks. Blinds were three-quarters drawn in the windows of the corner office, and she had the impression of a meeting taking place inside. She paid little attention, hurrying on towards her interview.

3

When lunchtime came, Andrew left the office alone. He was about to go into the sandwich shop over the road, but something stopped him. He didn't want to go back so soon, found it easier to think about the things that mattered out in the fresh air. The afternoon was glorious, a cool, fresh breeze on the heat, crowds of people drinking pints outside pubs. It was extraordinary how his state of mind jarred with the day; he saw nothing but happiness, felt nothing but tension.

He couldn't go on like this. The weekend had been a nightmare. Long silences in the flat and no way of breaking them – an occasional attempt at normal conversation, convincing as a nine-pound note. And it wasn't any better during the week, recently. Life with Rachel had settled into a pattern of uncertainty: he never knew when she'd be home, she never knew when he'd be home, and they never phoned each other at work. But finally, darkness would bring them to the same place, where they existed like unwelcome visitors in one another's lives . . .

He thought back to the conversation he'd had with Sophie earlier. He wanted to see her again very much – but that hadn't been the only reason he'd wanted to meet up with her tomorrow night. If he was honest with himself, *can't wait to see her* could also be directly translated into *don't want to go back to that bloody flat* – not wanting to spend another night wondering when Rachel would be back. Not even able to enjoy the peace of her absence, that could be shattered at any second by the sound of a key in the door. The return of unseen, invisible pressures, like the air before a thunderstorm.

He held those evenings up against time spent with Sophie. A

140

girl that he could understand, familiarity no longer breeding contempt as it had done with his girlfriends before Rachel. Easy chat in a pleasant bar, and nothing to worry about in the world.

How he longed to have those pre-Rachel days back. That freedom looked as enticing as a bottle of cold water to a man dying of thirst. He realised that he'd give a year's salary to be going back to a flat of his own. He'd have to tell Rachel it was over. He was moving out.

It wouldn't be easy. But it would only get harder the longer he left it. The situation would get more entangled and complicated, and he'd be more likely to let things go for the sake of a peaceful life. The idea that he could drift into a marriage and a future like this appalled him as never before, giving him the ruthlessness of urgency.

After all, he'd been having second thoughts for a long time, hadn't he? He'd been having second thoughts for *months*.

He checked his watch and turned back. He'd be late if he didn't return now. A tiny plane crawled across the luminous sky. He looked at it, seeing freedom, dreading the inevitability of telling Rachel. *The day after tomorrow*, he told himself. *I'll do it then* – putting it off as he always put off hated necessary tasks, creating a space in which to catch his breath, to steel himself to do what he had to.

4

When Rachel came into the Turk's Head at nine-fifteen, it was busier than it had been last time. A group of young men in pastel-coloured Ben Sherman shirts were gathered round the bar, noisy, interchangeable.

'For fuck's sake, Craig, it's your round,' one was saying. She headed past, hurrying towards the back, where Peter was waiting.

'Sorry I'm late,' she said, sitting down. 'I had to stay on at work.'

'It doesn't matter. I'd have waited all night for you.' He rose from his seat. 'What do you want?'

'A pineapple juice, please.'

He went to the bar. Her gaze strayed out of the window. It was beginning to get dark now, the quiet streets heavily shadowed. She watched until he came back, and handed her her drink.

'It's been too busy at work recently.' She spoke without thinking, thoughts of the office pressing on all sides. 'I'm working on a big pitch for Friday. It's turning into a nightmare.'

'Do you really care about it?'

'Of course I care about it. It's my job.'

'I think you're lying,' he said quietly. 'Not to me. To yourself. You're not like that.'

For the first time since she'd met him, she felt he'd misread her badly. It was unexpected and jarring, and she spoke a little too sharply. 'Like what?'

'Like the others in your office. I've seen them. I've heard them. I know the way they are.' He spoke almost casually, with throwaway hatred. 'They think there's nothing better in the world than selling people junk they don't need, and making money. They really can't understand how *meaningless* it is.'

'You think that?'

He nodded. 'And you do, too. You know you do.'

'I don't.' She broke off for a second, taking a deep breath. 'If that doesn't mean anything, what does?'

He shrugged. An entirely unexpected animosity had taken hold of Rachel, a sudden sense that he saw in her only what he wanted to. 'No, tell me,' she pressed. 'What do *you* think's important?'

'You're important. I'd do anything for you.'

It could have sounded corny beyond belief, but she was troubled by a bone-deep conviction that he meant every word. Across the table, his eyes were those of a zealot. 'What else?'

she asked, trying to hide her unease. 'Don't you care about *anything* else?'

The silence lasted some time before he spoke, his voice almost inaudible. 'When I was thirteen years old, my grandad gave me a gun. It's not licensed or anything. It's just there,' he said. 'Right after that, I joined a shooting club. They all thought it was just a hobby – couldn't understand why I didn't enter the competitions they had, told me I'd win every one. But I didn't care about their *trophies*. I just wanted to know how to use the gun. I left after two years. By then, I knew all I needed to.' Rachel watched him with dawning horror – the half-smile, the fugitive flicker in those large blue eyes. 'I've never used it,' he said. 'But I always keep it loaded. *That* matters. I care about *that*.'

It was as if she was seeing him for the first time. The normality of the surrounding world was very incongruous, the crowds at the bar, laughter from a nearby table. She had an overwhelming feeling that she'd strayed too far from home, into a dangerous area where certainties stopped existing. 'I'm sorry,' she said abruptly. 'This isn't right. Not for either of us.'

He watched her. Something in the quality of his silence demanded speech. 'I'm going out with someone. *Living* with him,' she said. She grabbed at Andrew's image in her mind, invoked him like a protective deity. 'I've got to go. I'm sorry.'

His expression didn't change. 'Can I give you my number?'

She was about to say no, but something stopped her; she didn't want to make him angry, she just wanted to go home. 'If you like.'

He scrawled on the back of a beer mat, handed it over. She took it, tucked it into her wallet. 'Thanks,' she said. 'Well, goodbye.'

Past the bar again, past the pastel-shirted lads, now clustering round the fruit machine. Out into the night. Approaching the parked MG, she found herself walking faster than there seemed any need for.

5

It was hot on the underground. A claustrophobic, sweaty heat, stirred by the occasional train. When Peter stepped on to the platform, he stood and looked across the tracks, at the posters. *Thomas Cook. Lambrini.* Beneath the rails, he saw mice moving.

He hadn't thought he'd ever tell anyone about Grandad. But of course, he'd tell her anything, would trust her with anything. He looked back to their meeting, and saw it cement their togetherness; he'd shared with her the only secret he'd ever have, the only secret he'd ever need.

His mother's father, his only real family apart from Mum, and Jessie. His father had walked out when he'd been four, and Grandma had been dead ten years when he was born. As a child, he'd gone to Grandad's flat just because it wasn't home – hating the old man's yellowing moustache and greying vests, the all-pervading smell of Woodbines and cheap brandy, but knowing it was infinitely preferable to the alternative. The alienation of laughter and ignorance, Jessie and her friends giggling round the telly, Mum chatting on the phone with any one of a dozen confidantes...

Grandad talked almost exclusively of war. At first, Peter wasn't particularly interested, but Grandad hadn't been in the class of storytellers that demanded interest from his audience. For Grandad, it was enough to have one. He talked about the injury that made him limp, about the mates who'd gone to fight with him – the ones who'd lived, the ones who'd died, the ones who'd been in wheelchairs ever since. Stories both enhanced and diminished by Grandad's incompetence as a narrator, the mundanity and repetition of horror.

Peter would always remember the restlessness of those long afternoons, as if each moment was spent on the brink of something momentous. Something that never came after all, that couldn't have been more out of place here; the shabby lounge, the smeary dark-wood surfaces crammed with bric-a-brac. Faded photographs in ugly, ornate gilt frames, and the windows always closed, stale smoke ingrained in cushions and curtains so they seemed to breathe it out themselves. The central heating up full blast. Even in winter, the air was stifling.

Still, Mum and Jessie never came here. Combined with the tingling, maddening sense of something unseen, that was enough to ensure his continuing presence: evenings, weekends, holidays with nobody but Grandad.

He'd been twelve, the day it had all changed. Sunday, late afternoon, autumn. The TV on as always, unwatched, showing an old black-and-white film. Grandad telling a story he'd heard several times before. He'd been paying little attention before Grandad broke off mid-monologue, looked at him closely.

Can you keep a secret, Pete boy?

Something intensely conspiratorial in the old man's voice made Peter's breath freeze in his throat. Never had the unseen something seemed closer. It was an effort to speak. *Sure.*

Grandad rose from his armchair, shuffled out of the room. Peter waited with his heart in his mouth, dreading disappointment. When Grandad came back in, he was carrying some kind of polished leather case. He sat back down, opened it slowly. Peter saw the pistol.

You're not to tell anyone about it, Pete boy. Put you in jail for things like that, they do – all licences and forms and what have you these days. Weren't none of that in my day. Took it off a dead Kraut soldier in Berlin, and no bugger knew a thing about it.

Fascination. Something hitherto unsuspected opening, unfolding. The twelve-year-old hand reaching out to touch cold metal. Far away, the crackle of the television, tinny voices that he barely heard at all.

He didn't think even Grandad had realised how much it meant to him. Grandad would never have guessed at the dreams he'd had, from that night on.

A distant murmur, then the train was rattling in. Peter

boarded with a handful of others, sat down in a carriage that was mostly empty. Turned his thoughts back to Rachel Carter. She might have said she didn't want to see him again, but he knew she didn't mean it. He knew her mind as well as his own. They were each other.

6

'Well,' said Sophie, 'I suppose I'd better get going.'

They were sitting together in Fusion again, at a table by the doors. Several dozen conversations were going on at full volume and at the same time, and they had to raise their voices considerably to make themselves heard.

'Damn – do you have to?'

'Afraid so.' The pause seemed a little hurt, accusing – she watched him regretfully across the table. 'I've got to be up at half six tomorrow to be in work on time. God, I hate these early starts.'

'Would you still have them in the other job?'

'No. I'd have to work Sundays, but it wouldn't bother me – I'd get another day off during the week.' Longing returned abruptly as her thoughts turned inwards. 'I hope I've got it. I really do.'

'You said it went well. The interview.'

'I *thought* it went well. I don't know anything for sure.' She took a deep breath, forced herself to smile. 'Oh well. I'll find out in the next few days.'

'Let me know when you hear something, won't you?'

'If you want me to.' His words startled her, delighting and unnerving both at once – implying something growing stronger between them too quickly. 'I will.'

They finished their drinks, and walked into the cooling summer night. Their journey to Farringdon station passed in awkward silence; as they walked, their hands brushed accidentally, and both drew away as if from a small electric shock. Her little laugh was involuntary and mirthless as a nervous reflex.

This time, they both went through the ticket barriers. Beyond them, two sets of stairs led down to opposite platforms, and a parting of the ways. They stood midway between the two flights, facing each other.

'I'll call you,' he said. 'Soon.'

'All right.' A noisy group of teenage girls thundered past them – the escalating rumble of a train drawing in, the mechanical warnings to *mind the gap*. 'I've had a really nice evening,' she said. 'Thank you very much.'

It was hard to know exactly what happened then. More people were coming past, and Andrew moved a little closer to her, to give them room. Then they were kissing. For a second, it could have been a chaste little peck, then it became something more – a long, hungry kiss that went on and on under the thin railway lights, a kiss that became oblivious to the world. His hands moved to her hair, hers to his.

She pulled away abruptly. 'I've got to go. I'll speak to you soon, okay?'

'Okay,' he said quietly. 'I'll be in touch.'

She walked down to her platform, and was barely aware that she did so. A train pulled in, and she stepped on in the same dreamlike state. She felt shocked, elated, disorientated, as if she'd just stepped off a big fairground ride. Something had been embarked on, the ultimate treachery – the memory of a kiss like a signed confession in her mind.

7

It was half past nine on Wednesday evening when Rachel decided to call it a day and go home. Sara and Christina had left maybe an hour ago. For the last few days, they'd been working like their lives depended on it, to a point where she'd all but forgotten her dislike of them. When you were this intent on a common goal, personalities stopped mattering; they shared the patriotism of BHN. Frantic phone calls to Production, Finance and Marketing, rushing down to the creatives' floor to check the finished visuals, calling eleventh-hour meetings with New Media – what could they do with the Powerpoint graphics in the space of forty-eight hours? Constant urgency, constant action. At any given second, they were racing for dear life.

For the first time in weeks, a treacherous little optimism had started nibbling at Rachel's mind. She fought to block it out, but day by day, it became harder to ignore; she found herself anticipating a relief that might never come after all. They weren't going to win any points for slick presentation, but the creative work might just be good enough to overcome that. It had been well worth waiting for Craig and Neil – they'd delivered the goods in grand style. And even if they didn't win, it might not be the disaster she'd dreaded; it wouldn't look good for her, but careers had survived worse.

She averted her mind from the mobile number in Andrew's pocket, from Nina and memories, from thoughts of Peter. Like a woman clinging to survival on a ledge, ignoring the hundred-foot drop had become life itself. She drove home on autopilot, cramming her mind with thoughts of nothing.

When she got in, the light in the living room told her Andrew was home. She took off her jacket in the hallway, came through. 'Hi,' she said. 'Good day?'

He turned to look at her. The TV was on quietly, playing the closing credits of *Friends*. Something in his eyes was all wrong.

'Look, Rachel,' he said. 'We need to talk.'

A lift in her stomach plummeted twenty floors. 'What about?'

'You'd better sit down,' he said. 'I'll turn that off.'

He reached for the remote as she sat. The picture shrunk

into a tiny white dot in the middle of the screen, then vanished. 'Well,' she said, 'what is it?'

'Rachel,' he said, 'I think we should split up.'

There had never been a silence like this, she thought distantly, never in the world.

'I'm sorry,' he said, 'but there's never going to be a good time to say it. It's just not working. Maybe it took living together to make us realise. You must know that, just as well as I do.'

Silence.

'I'll go back to Fulham tomorrow,' he said. 'Don't worry, I'm not going to stick you with the rent here – I'll pay it for the next three months, I'm happy to. That gives you plenty of time to find somewhere nice you can afford on your own. It's not fair if you have to hurry moving just because of money.'

She barely took in a word. When she spoke, her voice was flat, entirely emotionless. 'There's someone else, isn't here?'

His eyes moved awkwardly, as his shoulders did. 'It's not about that.'

'That's not an answer.'

'All right. In that case – I suppose there is.'

Silence. An echoing sense of nothing inside. 'Go tonight,' she said abruptly.

He looked at her. She heard her own dead voice like a stranger's. 'There's no point dragging it out. You can come back for your things tomorrow – they're safe here.'

The relief in his eyes was overwhelming. He spoke with something like gratitude. 'You know it's best,' he said. 'It's best for both of us.'

'Yes,' she said. 'I suppose it is.'

'We can still be friends, Rachel. I'd really like to stay in touch.'

'All right,' she said. 'That would be nice.'

'I'll come back for my things tomorrow evening. You've got my number in Fulham, if you need me.'

'I know,' she said. 'I have.'

There was nothing else to say. He left the room. She sat

149

statue-still and listened to him packing his overnight case. There was no other sound, and she could hear every detail. The thump of the case on the bedroom floor. The brief rattle of coat hangers. Footsteps moving between bedroom and bathroom, a light snapping on. Footsteps moving back again. The harsh and tiny rasp of a suitcase zipper. Footsteps approaching the living room.

'Goodbye,' he said formally, from the doorway. 'I'll phone you at work tomorrow.'

Then footsteps down the hallway, a second's pause. The front door opening. A tiny click as it closed behind him. She sat in the living room, not moving at all.

8

Images on a screen in her mind.

A party in Stamford Hill, Garbage blasting from the stereo, a glass of Diet Coke in her hand. Falling into conversation with a young man by the punchbowl. Making small talk, raising voices to make themselves heard.

You a friend of Steph's?

I work with her at Markson Vickery. We were on the graduate training programme together, last year.

I'm a mate of her brother's. My name's Andrew.

Smiling, shaking hands, appraising, flirtatious. Looking and seeing nothing out of the ordinary – nice-looking rather than handsome, tall, sandy-blond. The future predictable in her mind, an exchange of phone numbers, a few dates. A successor to Neil and Chris and Tony and Phil, a pleasant enough distraction from a job that wasn't that demanding yet. Not quite a relationship, nothing serious . . .

A corner table in a little Italian restaurant in Fulham, cosy, intimate, secluded. Candlelight and shadows, drinking coffee after dinner. A young couple holding hands across the table.

You know, it's been almost six months now, Rach...

Looking at him, realising he was right – a combination of shock and fear and happiness. She hadn't thought she'd ever be part of a Proper Couple, not at some deep level; hadn't been able to imagine herself sharing that kind of intimacy with anyone. But it had been almost six months now, and it seemed like no time at all. She felt she'd known him for ever. Watching him over the table, wondering if this was what they meant by *true love* – a phrase that had once seemed designed for greetings cards and Meg Ryan movies now taking on a previously unsuspected reality.

My God – I suppose it has.

A beautiful living room in an Oxfordshire family home that was never too elegant to be welcoming. Flames crackling in the grate, Christmas decorations twinkling in soft light, and oak beams slanting across the ceiling. Sitting with Andrew on the sofa, laughing at some joke of Helen's. Mrs Megson rising from her seat.

I must get a picture of you two. You make such a lovely couple...

Andrew's arm moving round her shoulder, reassurance in the pressure of his fingers. The flash illuminating a split second of heaven. She'd never known she could be this happy. That she could feel this secure with a man, this much a part of his life.

I'll send you a copy when I get this film developed. I'm sure it'll come out beautifully.

And finally, packing-crates in a Camden flat. A spacious living room, half furnished. Kneeling on the shiny parquet floor, unpacking various possessions from bubble-wrap. Andrew across the room, setting up the video.

Where do you think we should put this lamp?

How about on the mantelpiece? It'll look good there.

Putting it on the mantelpiece. He came over and kissed her. Before it became a full-scale embrace, the dizzying realisation that the past was over, her life had become perfect.

Rachel rose from her seat. She walked through the silent hallway and into the bathroom, snapping the light on. The absence of Andrew's tootbrush, toothpaste and mouthwash changed the look of everything. Pain moved inside her like some undersea creature below thick ice – a shape you guessed at rather than saw, blurred, unknowable.

Still, she was totally calm. Totally calm as she went back into the hallway and put her jacket on, as she left the flat, locking the door behind her. Totally calm throughout the drive to the all-night garage, the brief walk to the drinks section. She had the flat to herself tonight – that was as good a reason to drink again as any. There was no hysteria in her mind as she took down the half-bottle and carried it over to the till, as she got out her wallet and paid. Then she was home, pouring vodka over tonic and ice, taking the first long, deep sip, aware of no emotion at all.

It unsettled her, this inner emptiness. It felt like the brink of insanity.

9

Sophie had no idea when she'd hear about the job on the account handling floor, or how. Every e-mail had become both dreaded and longed for; every time the phone rang on her desk, she steeled herself for good and bad news at once.

But when her mobile began its muffled chirruping in the bag under her desk, she knew it would be Andrew.

'Sophie? How are you?'

'Not bad,' she said, then, lowering her voice, 'Still waiting to hear about that job. It's really starting to get to me.'

'You said you'd hear sometime this week, didn't you?'

'That's what they said at the time. Who knows?' Deliberately, she dragged her thoughts away. 'How are you, anyway?'

'All right. Me and Rachel split up last night. I've moved out.'

The words came out of nowhere, in a oddly business-as-usual tone. For seconds on end, she couldn't think of anything to say. 'What happened?' she managed at last. 'Did you have a row?'

'Nothing like that. Don't worry, it's not about us.' He took a deep breath. 'It's been on the cards quite a while. I just didn't want to tell you.'

'Why not?'

'It would have felt wrong,' he said squarely. 'Rachel had to know first. I owed her that much, at least.'

Sophie felt bewildered all over again; she'd initially imagined something mutual, or not even that, a curt dismissal on Rachel's own part. 'So you left her?'

'It wasn't that simple. I don't think she was any happier in the relationship than I was. Don't worry – it was all very civilised. No bad feelings. Maybe we'll even stay friends.'

'My God.' Sophie was still taking it in. She hated the extent of her joy, but couldn't deny it to herself – an insurmountable obstruction crumbling into dust as she watched, a clear road ahead. 'I don't know what to say.'

'I know. It feels weird to me too. It just had to be done.' For some seconds, neither said anything; when he spoke again, it was with deliberate good humour, a determined attempt at normality. 'Would you like to meet up again soon?'

'You know I would.' Across the office, she saw Jessie picking up her bag, heading over. It was almost half twelve. 'When do you think?'

'How about Friday night? Half seven at Fusion again?'

'That's fine.' It had become impossible to ignore Jessie hovering behind her back. 'Well,' she said, 'I'll see you there.'

She hung up with an overwhelming sense of disorientation as Jessie reached her desk. 'You coming for lunch, Soph?'

'Sure.'

They walked out of the office together. Suddenly, Sophie needed very badly to speak. 'Jessie, you know what I told you about my friend seeing that guy?'

Jessie nodded; Sophie hurried on. 'Well, I've got a bit of a surprise for you. It was me.' She took a deep breath. 'And he's single now. And he's lovely. And we're seeing each other.'

'That's terrific. I'm really pleased.' They stepped into the lift. 'And I've got a bit of a surprise for you.'

Sophie looked at her curiously. 'I knew it was you all the time.' Jessie grinned. 'Come on, Soph, it was *obvious*.' At first, Sophie was shocked, then couldn't help laughing. Jessie joined in before speaking again. 'Can we go to Boots after the sandwich shop? I've got to get some conditioner.'

10

It felt like bereavement, before the tears. A sense of unreality hung over everything. She existed in her body like a disinterested passenger, was aware of it moving and speaking – the words didn't make much sense to her, but some mechanism kept them coming, knew what was expected. Her exhaustion didn't seem to affect that mechanism, nor did her hangover.

'We'll have a run-through in the boardroom later,' she was saying. 'I've booked it from three till six.'

Bright sunlight through the window hurting her eyes, Sara and Christina sitting across from her in her office. Blinds drawn across the glass partition, the sound of her own voice. 'There's no denying that we've had a few problems,' she was saying, 'but we'll just have to do the best we can. For all we know, it'll be all right on the night.' Extraordinarily, they were smiling; she was smiling back at them. 'We've been putting in some long hours lately, and I'd like to thank you both for that,' the voice went on. 'Our hard work might just pay off tomorrow morning.'

'Shame we're presenting first,' Sara said. 'I *hate* early starts.'

Laughter. Rachel recognised its slightly wild quality from the Fanta pitch – how it felt just before crunch-time, a kind of panicky backstage camaraderie. It drifted into her like a memory from a former life; she heard her own laughter joining it, and felt nothing. 'Well, even so, we should be there well before we present,' she was saying. 'We go into their boardroom at nine, but I'd like us to meet in reception at half eight.'

'Where's the nearest tube?' asked Christina.

'There isn't one, I'm afraid. The nearest railway station's Redbridge – it's about fifteen minutes' train-ride from Victoria. It should be easy enough to get a taxi to the Fiat building, once you're there,' said Rachel. 'I'm driving, but you'd better check train times this afternoon.'

When they'd gone, Rachel checked her watch. Half twelve, she saw. Peter would have come and gone. Still, she kept the blinds closed. Sitting at her desk, she looked at the photograph: dazzling smiles, oak beams, arm round shoulder and Christmas tree rising in the background. It was like torture on anaesthetised flesh – she looked, and couldn't understand why she felt dead.

At quarter to one, the phone shrilled.

'Hi, Rachel, it's me,' said Andrew. 'Haven't called at a bad time, have I?'

Again, the sense of nothing; she saw the thumbscrews tightening as if on someone else. 'No,' she said. 'I'm on my own here.'

'I just called to let you know I'll be coming round for my things this evening. There's nothing that won't fit in my car. The furniture and stuff we got together – that's yours. I'll just take what I need.'

How desperate he was to break free. She had a strong sense that he'd have given her anything in exchange for an amicable split, no guilt, no regrets. 'I'll probably be round about seven,' he said. 'Will you be in?'

'I'll probably have to stay late. I expect I'll miss you.'

'Well.' A moment's uneasy silence. 'I'll leave a cheque for next month's rent. I'll send the rest on when I get paid – I haven't got that much in my account right now.'

'Thank you,' she said quietly. 'That's very kind.'

'It's nothing. It's only fair.' The pause seemed to drag out for ever. 'Well,' he said eventually, 'I'll see you, Rachel.'

'All right,' she said. 'Goodbye, Andrew.'

She hung up knowing that she'd never see him again.

11

When she got home that night, her key turned in the lock to silence and darkness. She put the hall light on, locked and bolted the door behind her.

The living room was virtually as it had been. Only the photographs on the mantelpiece were gone, maybe a quarter of the CDs in the five-foot-tall rack, a handful of the DVDs by the television unit. There was no real change at all; there was all the change in the world.

The ache struck then, for the first time. A dull pain somewhere in the pit of her stomach, almost ignorable.

In the bedroom, everything looked exactly the same, till she opened the wardrobe door and saw he'd cleared out his half completely. You'd never have known there'd been a man living here; everything was hers. He'd put her jackets and full-length coats in the empty half. She looked, and saw his mind working an hour or more ago, what he thought he knew about what she loved. Tidiness. Order. Everything in its place.

The pain intensified.

She closed the wardrobe doors and went into the kitchen. Everything was where it had been that morning. She looked in cupboards and saw what she always saw – the same plates, the same pots, the same wok for stir-fries. The same spices,

156

and herbs, and sauces. She saw he'd even left his jar of Nutella.

Andrew standing at the counter in the mornings, spreading Nutella thickly on toast, leaving the jar on the side with the lid off; the crumbs, the Virgin Radio breakfast show he always listened to. Tiny details did what the photograph by her desk hadn't been able to, smashing through the reservoir of her apathy. One moment, she was standing blank-eyed and statue-still; the next, crying helplessly as the enormity of loss hit home. She grabbed the jar of Nutella from the shelf and threw it across the kitchen with all her strength. It smashed against the adjacent wall and richocheted to the floor, bleeding thick brown.

She leant against the counter, crying harder than ever; felt fury combining with agony as the seconds passed, then felt raw, burning hatred join the chorus. As suddenly as she'd understood what his loss really meant, she understood the part Sophie had played in it. What she must have told Andrew to make him see her differently, to make him want to leave. He'd know about the promenade-and-booze years now, the baby she'd never had, whose father she'd never known. He'd know about the suicide attempt.

He wouldn't know what had caused it all. That was one thing Sophie would never have told him. But it all seemed inextricably linked in her mind; cause and result, trigger and injury. The shameful things that would ruin her in people's eyes for ever – the things that would end anyone's love for her, that could shatter a long-standing state of emotional stability as instantly and irrevocably as a window-pane.

Of course, they wouldn't say so. But they'd be disgusted, as disgusted as she'd been by herself. Anyone decent would be appalled, see her as contaminated by what she'd done, by what had happened to her. A chain of events that had all begun in Acacia Avenue . . .

You're so efficient, Rachel, Nina had said delightedly, long ago, before that summer. In another life. *So responsible. I wouldn't be surprised if you were Prime Minister when you grow up—*

But afterwards, it had all changed.

12

What's the matter, Rachel? You don't seem like yourself at all lately – ever since you got back from the Townsends'.

Couldn't tell her mother. Had to hide it away. Nina's love for her was built on an image of the girl she'd been before – the innocent girl, the girl grown-ups respected, the girl who always got everything right. The idea of her knowing the truth was appalling. She wouldn't just be disappointed, she'd be *devastated.*

And Nina would never look at her the same way, if she knew. Rachel would never see that love in her eyes again. That admiration.

It's nothing, Mum. I just had a row with Sophie. We're not talking to each other any more.

Recurrent nightmares. The constant pressure of secrecy. A suspicion that any conversation could give her away; if she let herself forget what she was hiding, she might somehow reveal—

When she was fourteen, she fell in with a new crowd at St Andrew's Secondary. A group of girls who had nothing in common with her old clean-cut friends. But *she* had nothing in common with them any more; their innocence alienated her, made her feel dirty, inferior. Her new friends were the bad-news crowd – some shiny-faced, the rest inexpertly caked in make-up. They smoked behind the bike shed and gossiped about shagging, and talked about nothing that mattered. It soothed her that they didn't seem to know or care who she really was, what she was really feeling. The joylessness of their rebellion was overwhelming – they trudged towards oblivion like a busy Monday morning.

Coming down the promenade tonight, Rach? Keith and that from Underlyme Grammar's going to be there. They're bringing some booze down—

The promenade at night. Eight or nine of them pressing into the peeling paint and carved initials of one of the shelters, the wind blowing a diffuse mist of rain. Waves crashing down in the darkness, past the deserted beach. Cupped hands round guttering matches, a two-litre plastic bottle doing the rounds—

You finished with that yet, Rach?

And boys in the group, of course. Some their age, some a little older – greasy-haired and biker-booted, their conversation entirely composed of swear-words and barely audible monosyllables. In Rachel's mind, they were all the same. And when one of them took her down a side alley one night and tried to make a kiss into something more, she didn't stop him. She wasn't a virgin anyway, might as well seek out sex on her own. By sleeping around, she could make it something throwaway, something meaningless; prove that the events of Acacia Avenue hadn't really mattered.

Oh, there was a good time to be had in the night – the flickering rain and the cheap white cider, the deserted alleyway in the small hours, the inevitability of the furtive shag with another virtual stranger. And if her grades had taken a nose-dive since that summer and she wasn't exactly head girl material any more, who cared? There was more to life than school, wasn't there? There was this.

And behind it all, the terror of something lost, wandering in a strange and unknown land. Driving her on to more booze-fuelled oblivion, more nights on the promenade, more one-night stands you could hardly even dignify with the name. Sometimes the boys she went with used protection, sometimes they didn't. She couldn't have cared less. She knew people were talking behind her back at school, and she couldn't have cared less about that, either. Still, she kept as much of it from Nina as she possibly could – making up good news from school, staying round at her mates' houses when she'd been drinking. More than anything, she feared Nina discovering the promiscuity, somehow tracing it back to source.

Then, when she was fifteen years old, her period hadn't come—

Rachel sat at the kitchen table and poured herself another vodka tonic. She'd bought the bottle on the way back from work, pre-empting a pain whose strength she hadn't been able to imagine. She supposed she should clear up the smashed Nutella jar in the corner, and stared at it for some time, wondering whether to or not. No. It could wait. She raised the glass to her lips, and drank deeply.

You're stupid to drink tonight, an inner voice howled. *It's the pitch first thing tomorrow, you need to be on form.* But it was strangely muted, as if it had filtered in from a distant room. Tonight, she needed anything that could anaesthetise her, make her forget Andrew wasn't here any more. Make her stop crying. She sat in the silent kitchen, poured again, and drank again until life was forgotten.

13

She woke up gradually. She was lying on top of the bed, fully clothed. At first she was aware of nothing but nausea and bewilderment, then the pain came back, sinking into her with rusty metal teeth. Andrew had left. He'd taken his things yesterday.

And the Fiat pitch was *this morning.*

In an instant, she was fully awake, sitting up. Her gaze snapped over to the alarm clock. Six thirty. She hadn't set the alarm, she saw with fresh horror – luck alone had woken her in time.

No time to think about how out-of-control she must have been to forget, to crash out on a made bed wearing blouse and skirt and tights. She rushed into the bathroom, stripped off and got into the shower. The cool water should have been refreshing, but made her shiver like a woman in the grip of a high fever. She was convinced she was about to throw up, and stood unmoving under the running water, feeling her stomach slowly unclench like a fist.

She towelled off and went back into the bedroom, to the wardrobe that only contained womenswear. She selected and changed into one of her favourite skirt suits. At the dressing-table mirror, she made up carefully, but the sight of herself was terrifying as never before. The golden morning sunlight that should have flattered had become as stark as striplights – she saw pallor and dark circles, a clearly legible sickness in every line of her face.

No need to hide the bottle she'd left on the kitchen table last night. When raging thirst drove her in towards the fridge, she just averted her eyes, pouring herself a long glass of orange juice and draining it in one gulp. There was a fly buzzing round the Nutella jar on the floor, but there was no time to do anything about it. She'd clear it up when she got back. She had to get going.

Into the MG; she started the engine and switched on the radio out of habit. The DJ's cheerful inanities kicked in mid-word. It was a glorious morning, already nearly hot enough to sunbathe. Trees cast ink-black shadows, and the breeze from the air-con was light and refreshing. Still, she felt clammy and jittery, at once ultra-tense and somehow dislocated from the world around her; she could feel an elastic band pulling tighter and tighter in her mind, preparing to snap.

Coming out of Camden Town, she turned a corner and squealed to a halt. The southbound lane was jammed solid. Nothing but glittering metal ahead, as far as the eye could see; the cars in front of her might as well have been parked.

Impossible to tell what was holding them up. Rachel knew that jams like this were often as easy to untie as a Boy Scout's knot – a quick yank *here* and *here* and it was all back to normal. But as five minutes' standstill turned to ten, and ten to fifteen, nothing showed any sign of changing. The DJ's cheerful voice had become maddening. *Nothing to worry about,* the tone implied chummily, *it's a beautiful day in the capital, and we're all doing fine.*

It's about fifteen minutes' train-ride from Victoria, she'd said to Sara and Christina yesterday. *I'd like us to meet in reception at half eight.*

'And that was Christina Aguilera,' the DJ announced. 'Coming up to five past eight, and—' Panic began to surge into Rachel's thoughts, like something on the brink of hysteria – a trapped bird flapping wildly in a cage, battering itself against solid bars. No movement. Glinting metal. The car in front was an elderly Metro. A cornucopia of small stuffed animals smirked out at her through its rear window. A faded bumper sticker read BABY ON BOARD.

Jesus Christ, I am going to be late. The thought came with swooning terror as the seconds ticked away on the dashboard clock. It was then that the taut elastic in her mind snapped, a change as sudden and tangible as a broken bone.

There was a side street leading off the road directly across from her, beyond the opposing lane. A jerky three-point turn that narrowly avoided smashing into the Metro, and she was swerving out towards the side street, straight into the flow of oncoming traffic. A Transit van slammed its brakes on just in time. Horns screamed, but she barely heard them. She was late and she was *late* and *she was late,* and she *had to be there on time—*

Hammering down narrow residential streets, not quite knowing where she was going, not caring. As long as she kept going. That was all that mattered. A near miss with an Audi and a Shogun and a Mini in quick succession, and she was turning back on to the main road, and in the rear-view mirror, she saw—

Flashing blue lights. Right behind her.

It was like deafening music turning into silence with the press of a button. The sight cut her hysteria off instantly. Dull, apathetic horror rushed in to replace it. *This can't be happening to me. Not now.*

She pulled over. The police car stopped behind her. In the rear-view mirror, she saw the policeman getting out, approaching. He was in his middle twenties and skinny; long lines of nose and jaw, shaving rash. He looked officious, indifferent and depressed all at once. She pressed the button to wind the window down. He looked in at her, and saw anyone.

'Excuse me, madam, do you know what speed you were travelling at?'

No answer to that. She shook her head. She saw him looking at her more closely, seeming to take in her pallor, the sick, inexplicably dishevelled look that she'd seen for herself in the mirror.

'Would you step out of the car, please?'

The words might as well have been a Latin mass, learned by heart, barely understood; he spoke the stock phrase without emphasis. She unbuckled her seatbelt and stepped out on to the pavement, closing the door behind her. He had something in his hand.

'Would you mind blowing into the bag for me, please, madam?'

Oh, Jesus – the near-empty bottle in the kitchen flashed behind her eyes. She had no idea what time she'd finished drinking last night, what might or might not remain in her system. Through the open driver's window, she could hear the DJ's voice. 'And with the time coming up to eight twenty,' he was saying, 'here's a classic from Robbie—'

Nothing else for it. She blew in the bag as instructed, saw people slowing slightly on their way to work, turning their heads to look. She'd stared like that herself, on occasion, but it suddenly seemed grotesquely prurient. She handed the breathalyser back in silence, and watched him reach for his radio, mutter into it words she couldn't quite catch.

'If you'd like to accompany me to the station, madam,' he said at last. 'It's the law that we give you a second test at once. The first shows that you're over the legal alcohol limit.'

She stared at him blankly. 'Am I under arrest?'

He nodded.

'Excuse me, but can I make a quick phone call? There's someone I have to get in touch with.'

She was clinging on to the last vestiges of composure with a great effort as they came through the double doors of Camden police station. In the reception, she saw exhausted-looking pot-plants, orange plastic chairs, a notice-board crammed with printed flyers.

'They'll be worried,' she told the silence beside her. 'I have to let them know where I am.'

'I'm sorry, madam, but it's the law that you have a second breathalyser test right away. First things first.'

Her eyes flicked over to the round institutional clock above the reception desk. Just past eight forty-five; the idea that this meant nothing at all to him suddenly enraged her. 'Look, I'm supposed to be leading a *pitch*, for Christ's sake! It's *important*!'

'I'm very sorry, madam, but so is this. I don't think you're taking the situation quite seriously enough.'

His voice had cooled twenty degrees, and told her instantly that she'd antagonised him, that she'd handled it all wrong. She should have been more diplomatic, she realised – she just couldn't think straight. They went up a wide flight of stairs. Two policemen passed them on the way down, deep in conversation. She saw them without really seeing them at all. Part of her couldn't believe this was happening; another part of her could believe it only too well.

Sara and Christina restless in the Fiat reception, anxious eyes returning time and again to the doors. *Rachel's got to be here any minute*, Sara said in her mind. *Where the hell's she got to?*

Couldn't ask to call them again. Not now.

In a small, barely furnished room on the first floor, she took the breathalyser test again. This time a middle-aged woman supervised it, while the indifferent young man with the shaving rash stood beside her. When it was done, and the room was silent, Rachel looked out of the window. She could see the police station car park, the mundane comings and goings beyond it, the world intent on another working day.

'The second test also shows you to be over the legal limit,' the woman said at last, then, wearily, as something known by heart, she read out the charge: driving with excess alcohol, punishable by a year's loss of licence, minimum, a possible fine of at least a thousand pounds.

Rachel dreaded the answer, but had to know. 'Am I still detained here?'

'No. You have to stay with us while we fill out the paperwork and arrange a date for your court appearance. After that, you're free to leave.'

She fought for the right tone of voice. 'Do you know roughly how long that will take?'

'About half an hour,' said the woman briskly. 'You'll have to leave your car with us, but you can pick it up first thing tomorrow.'

Rachel barely took in any of the last sentence. *About half an hour.* She managed to roll her sleeve up unobtrusively, catching a glimpse of her watch-face from the corner of her eye. Ten past nine.

She couldn't keep the ragged edge out of her voice as she addressed them. 'Look, can I make a phone call while I'm waiting? There's someone I really have to get in touch with.'

'Sure thing.' Without the stock formalities, the young policeman's voice was normal, even pleasant – it held all the relief of plain clothes. 'There's a payphone in reception.'

'It's all right,' said Rachel. 'I'll use my mobile.'

Out in the hallway, she stood as the middle-aged police-woman watched her from the doorway. She only had Sara's mobile number with her. She dialled it quickly, with only the vaguest idea what she wanted to say. The line was engaged.

Rachel pressed the button to hang up, and tried again straight away. No change. She stood where she was, phone mute in hand, breathing deeply, trying to forget about the woman watching her. She was a few seconds away from trying a third time when the phone shrieked in her hand, almost stopping her heart. She answered in a breathless, strangled voice.

'Hello?'

'Where the *fuck* are you?'

It was Diane.

15

'Well – you've got the job,' said Lisa. 'They left it to me to pass on the news.'

They were sitting in Lisa's little corner office. Sophie had known she'd hear one way or the other as soon as Lisa had invited her in. She sat and stared for a long heartbeat, over-joyed. 'Congratulations,' Lisa went on. 'I thought you'd get it.'

'That's terrific,' said Sophie slowly. 'When do I start?'

'The Monday after next. You should be getting a new job description and contract through the internal mail some time today. Just sign a copy of the contract and hand it back to Personnel over the next few days.'

Sophie couldn't quite keep the smile off her face. 'Sure. I'll do that.'

'I'm glad it's good news. And you're obviously pleased about it.' Lisa smiled back at her. 'I think it's a great opportunity for you, Sophie. It's not an overnight stepping-stone, by any means, but it's a very good place to start, if you're serious about a long-term career here.'

'I know,' said Sophie, 'and I am.'

Back at her desk, she dialled Andrew's number.

'Guess what?' she said quietly. 'I've got the job.'

'That's great! Congratulations! Why don't we have a meal somewhere nice tonight, to celebrate?'

'That'd be terrific,' she said. 'I'd love to.'

'I'll book somewhere. Call you back in half an hour or so,' he said. 'And well done.'

Sophie hung up. Happiness and restlessness and wonderment filled her all at once. This was, she realised, the dream she'd had on her way into Waterloo, in a different life. She felt like a real insider in this city, at last.

16

'Well.' Diane's voice was brittle with throwaway menace. 'This had better be good.'

Diane's office was entirely separate from the main open-plan space, the walls solid. A distant part of Rachel was glad this exchange would take place away from Kate and the others, where no raised voices could filter through to them. Still, the claustrophobia was overwhelming; there was nowhere to look except at Diane, and she didn't want to look at Diane at all.

'I couldn't help it!' she burst out. 'I was in an accident!'

'You'd better be able to prove that. You're going to have to produce all the paperwork, you know.' A moment's deadly silence. 'This isn't something I'm just going to take on trust, Rachel. When Sara rang me from the Fiat building, I literally couldn't believe it.'

'I tried to phone her from the police station, the first chance I had! They wouldn't let me make the call at first, and—'

Rachel broke off mid-sentence, realising that that wouldn't have been the case if she'd just been in an accident. But of course, it didn't matter anyway; she wouldn't be believed till she could produce paperwork that didn't exist. She didn't know whether Diane had noticed the slip. It would have been impossible for her to look any more accusing.

'They couldn't present, of course,' Diane said at last. 'Asked me what to do on the phone. If I hadn't been there to tell them, they might have gone into that boardroom anyway – a couple of bog-standard account handlers who don't know jack shit about presenting.' Diane's voice rose with appalling suddenness. 'And they'd have been laughed out of the fucking building! This is Fiat we're talking about, Rachel, not fucking Disneyland!'

'Can't we go back and explain to them?' Rachel heard her voice tremble, realised she was on the edge of tears. 'We could reschedule the presentation – I'm sure they'd understand. We could let them know what happened, and—'

'Oh, for Christ's sake.' The quiet dismissal was contemptuous beyond words, more terrible than her earlier rage. 'Wake up, Rachel. Thanks to you, we're the agency that can't even pull its finger out for the pitch date. How much credibility do you think we'll have with them right now?'

Rachel couldn't bring herself to look directly at Diane; she fixed her eyes on a photograph on Diane's desk. A couple of little kids, plump, blonde, giggling into the camera. The incongruity was bizarre; a wedding band on an executioner's hand. The feared and hated senior account director watched her coldly across the desk.

'We made a big mistake when we promoted you,' she said at last. 'You're not ready for it.'

The crucial last word was *yet*; Rachel felt its omission like a hard punch to the stomach. 'I haven't got anything else to say to you,' Diane said at last. 'You might as well go back to your office.'

She did, inexplicably terrified of passing Sara and Christina. But they weren't at their desks, and the main office was mostly empty. Once inside her own, she shut the door, drawing the blinds at the glass partition. Professionalism demanded that she call an explanatory meeting with Sara and Christina as soon as they came back, but she somehow couldn't. It would feel too strange, and she dreaded their eyes on her. An odd stillness had descended in her mind, a sense that all activity had become pointless.

She was living out the last of her time here. There was no question in her mind that Diane would get her thrown out in the next few weeks. Her powerful champion had become a powerful enemy. Diane's decision to promote the star of the Fanta pitch, Diane's credibility dealt a body-blow by this disaster, Diane's twenty-twenty judgement abruptly called into question. You didn't need to see that much of Diane Robinson to know how she'd react to the situation.

If I didn't think you were up to it, Rach, she'd said long ago, *I'd never have fought like I did to get you promoted . . .*

Almost twelve noon. She couldn't decide whether the gnawing in the pit of her stomach was hunger or nausea. It would be a good idea to get some fresh air and a sandwich, but at the thought of going out, fear seized her. Sara and Christina might be back at their desks now, and she'd have to pass them on her way to the lifts. She imagined them gossiping at the centre of an agog group, watching her with judgemental, sneering eyes as she hurried past.

And then, of course, she'd have to come back.

They could be there, they could be out. The only way to tell was to open the blinds – but if they *were* there, she'd have to close them again straight away. And they'd notice the movement. They'd *laugh* at the movement. They'd know what was going through her mind. In the end, she stayed in her office with the blinds down, hoping Peter would knock despite that, knowing he wouldn't. Trying to remind herself that it was better she didn't see him.

I always keep it loaded, he'd said, and she'd had a shivering sense of something dark beyond expression; something hungry in his voice, a kind of lust he'd never displayed towards her. *That* matters. I care about *that . . .*

She stayed in that soundless, shuttered world all afternoon. What little she had to do was easily handled over the phone and e-mail. Nobody knocked. As the house passed, the nausea-edged hunger intensified till she was weak with it, and she still didn't dare, didn't quite dare open the door or the blinds. She looked out of the window and saw people coming and going three floors down, strolling through streets flooded with sunshine. Friday afternoon, the time to be anticipating dinner with the man you loved, easy conversation, the end of another successful week.

We made a big mistake when we promoted you. You're not ready for it.

Would you blow into the bag, please, madam?

Rachel, I think we should split up.

Turning back, she saw the photograph by her computer as if for the first time. She took it off her desk and put it into the waste-bin with the slow, drugged movements of a sleepwalker.

By six o'clock, she knew Sara and Christina must have gone home – they never stayed late on Fridays. By seven o'clock, she was sure enough of it to make a move. A small, bitter relief came as she opened the door at last. The office was empty. She could leave unwatched.

She got the lift down to reception and stepped out. Kate was standing outside one of the other lifts, smiling and laughing.

Talking to Sophie.

'Guess what, Rach?' Kate called. 'Sophie's going to be joining us on our floor next week— Hey, are you okay?'

Rachel looked at Sophie for a second that lasted a lifetime. Looking back across the years, she saw her in a back garden, Acacia Avenue in July, those words behind the shed—

You're lying!

Hatred came in a tidal wave. In a split second, it had become all she contained. Her heartbeat was hammering in her ears as she walked past them without a word, out of the high-gloss reception, into the warm, crowded, sociable evening.

It was then that the idea came. It entered her mind like the stab of an icepick.

17

Eight thirty. Peter was sitting up in his bedsit. He could hear the faint murmur of the television from next door, muffled, pounding chart music from the unofficial common-room as the women cackled their interminable laughter, and knew nothing. He thought about going for a walk.

He felt this restlessness more and more recently – an electric feeling he associated with Grandad's flat all those years ago, the sense of something as yet unseen, waiting for the right moment to reveal itself. An unreachable itch at the back of his mind becoming close to unbearable. It was as if his contact with Rachel had been the catalyst: two months ago, these solitary walks had been a well-loved fantasy; now, they were as essential to his life as she was.

He heard the phone ringing in the hallway downstairs, a door opening, footsteps. One of the strangers answering. Then his voice again, surprised, calling up the stairs. 'Peter? It's for you.'

Rachel, of course. There'd been no doubt in his mind that he'd hear from her soon. He went down, had a brief glimpse of a bedsit door closing behind a stranger's back. Alone in the shadowed hallway, he lifted the receiver.

'Hello, Peter? It's me, Rachel.'

She only ever told him what he knew already. There was nothing else she could do, he realised, when they were the same. 'How are you?' she went on. 'Having a good evening?'

His thoughts turned to the night outside. 'In a way,' he said. 'I expect I will do.'

'That's good.' A strange, charged pause – the electric, waiting feeling stronger than ever in his mind. 'Listen, I was wondering. Could you meet me tomorrow night? There's something I want to talk to you about.'

'All right,' he said. 'The Turk's Head again, at eight?'

'That's fine. That's great.' Another ambiguous silence before she spoke again. 'Well, I'll see you then.'

'Goodbye, Rachel,' he said.

Back up the stairs to his room. The muffled sounds through the wall and the floor had taken on an unreal quality, fuzzy and distorted. Rachel's voice returned to him with perfect crystal clarity. *There's something I want to talk to you about.* He didn't know what *that* meant. But specific curiosity had become as alien to him as fear; he'd find out tomorrow, that was enough.

He would go out. He had to go out. A little voice in his mind always told him that these excursions were potentially very dangerous, but each time he went for one, that voice grew a little quieter. Tonight, it was barely audible, easily ignorable on the outskirts of his thoughts.

Even here, he'd had to conceal his treasure carefully. He knelt on the floor by the chest of drawers. The bottom drawer was empty. He lifted it out as quietly as he could. The dark-brown leather holster was underneath. Opening it, he extracted the pistol. He made sure the safety catch was on, although it always was when he handled it. Double-checking was the first of many things he'd learned at the gun club; he recalled his instructor's confused, vaguely accusing voice with perfect clarity. *You really ought to enter the competitions, you know, Peter. You're one of the best shots we've ever had here.*

They hadn't known much about him, really. But then, he hadn't wanted them to.

Tucking the pistol into the pocket of his jeans, he went to the wardrobe, and put on the baggy sweater he always wore on these nights, obscuring the bulge at his hip. It hung almost to his knees, but much stranger things were the height of fashion. Too hot for the time of year, too. It didn't matter. Most people noticed nothing, and even the few who did wouldn't understand what they were seeing.

He needed these nights, recently. Nights defined not by what he did, but by what he didn't do . . .

He stepped out on to the landing. The pounding chart

music was louder here, the door to the communal room open a few inches. It gave an overwhelming impression of smoke and lager cans en route to mouths, a sordid and ugly clutter he hated more than anything – the cackling voice as he moved closer underscoring the mindless disco beat like a bass line. 'So I reckon he's mucking her about,' an unseen woman was confiding, 'and I said to her, he's just taking the piss—'

He didn't get the pistol out of his pocket and snap the safety catch off and step in, door banging hard against the wall as they looked round in a second of dawning terror. Didn't get the talking woman with one bullet and a total stranger with another a second later, didn't see an imagined array of cosmetics on the dressing table shatter one after the other like clay ducks in a shooting gallery as he aimed and fired, again and again and again. Didn't kill the stereo with the last bullet, see that hated music silenced in a sharp, explosive pop that sent sparks flying. He didn't walk out, leaving the silent bedsit like a slaughterhouse before heading down the stairs.

He didn't stop to reload in the hallway, before leaving the house.

Out in the night, the streets were thronging with Friday-night crowds, heading to bars and between bars – big groups of shrieking girls in miniskirts and thigh-boots and bra-tops, big groups of lads in Top Shop and Ben Sherman and Ralph Lauren from the market, hair stiff and shiny with gel under the streetlights. Loud, noisy and interchangeable, wearing their shrill and ersatz happiness like badges of membership to some pitiful club.

'Yeah, she's fuck-off horny,' a skinny red-haired youth was saying to his mates as Peter passed them. 'Reckon she's well out of your league, mate.' Peter didn't take the safety off again as he took the pistol out for a second time, and he didn't aim and fire; the bullet didn't catch the youth half an inch above his prominent Adam's apple, the youth wasn't clutching at his throat before any of his mates understood what had happened.

Peter walked on.

It was what he'd fallen in love with back in Grandad's flat, as the holster opened for the first time. Something he'd recognised from movies and TV, something he'd never previously related to his own life. The idea that this small piece of metal could change everything; the potential destruction of everything he hated was something he could hold in his hand.

Still, the idea that he *could* wasn't quite enough, as it had been only a month ago. Each time he did this, it became a little less satisfying, had taken on the unfulfilling delight of an appetiser. On the last few occasions, he'd found himself wanting so much more, and never had that been more true than tonight.

It was half two in the morning when his key turned in the front door. These nights out did strange things with time. Moonlight illuminated the hallway, the stairs that he ascended quietly. Back in his bedsit, he extracted the bottom drawer, replaced the gun with infinite care. As he slid the drawer back, the electric tingle of the unknown flooded his mind – what his goddess wanted from him, what she had to tell him tomorrow night.

18

You can't be doing this. You must have lost your mind to even think about it...

Rachel ignored the aghast inner voice as best she could. It had been screaming at her all day, all evening – the voice of someone who'd never been forced to understand what hatred meant, the voice of convention, reason, normality. It simultaneously unsettled and antagonised her, making her realise how appalling her plans really were, and how little choice she had.

Through the double doors of the Turk's Head, noise and smoke and music hit her like a fist. The pub was thronging with a trendy young Saturday-night crowd, pressing round the bar and the pool table, shrieking with laughter. She wasn't sure whether Peter would have been able to sit down, but as she moved through the crowd and towards the back of the pub, she saw he had – he was by the window again, alone at a small round table for two. An island of silence seemed to surround him as she approached, and nobody gave him a second glance.

More then ever, his strangeness unsettled her. But it was that quality she'd come here in search of.

'Hello, Peter,' she said, sitting down.

'Rachel.' He rose from his seat. 'What do you want to drink?'

The predictable ritual would change soon, would stray into territory she'd never seen before in her life. Knowing it, she clung to what she'd seen and done before, as if for warmth. 'A pineapple juice, please.'

Pounding music from the jukebox filled her mind. Her gaze panned across an infinity of laughing strangers, and she felt normality unwinding around her like the last few turns of cotton on a reel.

Then he was coming back. He handed her her drink and sat down.

'So what do you want?'

It sounded like antagonism, but she knew it wasn't. She saw that darting something in his eyes again, gone before she could put a name to it. She ignored the warning voice in her head with a vast effort of will – it clung to her like a fractious child, shrieking in her ear as she fixed determined eyes straight ahead.

'When we last met, you said you'd do anything for me.' She spoke quietly, leaning closer to him across the table. 'Did you mean that?'

'Of course I did. You know that.'

He said it as if it was nothing but a simple fact. The tone emboldened her, and she pressed on. 'So if I wanted you to do something – anything at all – you'd do it?'

He only nodded. Their faces were almost touching now, and the crowds around them had ceased to exist. The voice was deafening in her mind, howling like a fire bell. She tore herself away from it, and steeled herself to leap into the unknown. She said, 'I want you to kill someone.'

Book Five

Found this book in a drawer just now when I was looking for some paper. I'd forgotten all about it. Went back through it and can't believe I never threw it out. I will, after this. Just need to get my thoughts out somehow because they're all tangling up in themselves and chasing round in circles and I don't know where to start and

You know, I haven't written in it since 1988, nearly two years ago. Kind of got out of the habit after that – every time I thought I might, I remembered all the other stuff that's in it. Sounds weird, but I didn't want to see that stuff written down. If I didn't look at it, I thought I could just about forget what happened that summer, and it seemed like everything might be okay then. I'd changed, but people do change when they're teenagers, it didn't have to mean anything bad.

But last night, when I knew for sure it was true, I had the nightmare again, the one I had for months after they came back to Acacia Avenue, and I came back here, and the autumn term started. It felt real, like it always did then. I was lying in my own bed, sleeping, then the door creaked open, and I saw Uncle Brian's shadow in the door when I woke up—

Anyway. Trying to get my head together, but it's hard. Thoughts going all over the place. Maybe I want them to be all over the place. Don't want to think about being pregnant, even now I've done the test and know I am.

My period hasn't come for the last three months. I just ignored it. I know it doesn't make sense, but I kept thinking that if I ignored it, it couldn't be true. I can't explain how it gets in your head when you're that scared. Kept thinking I'd

*have to tell Mum, knowing I couldn't. She used to be so
proud of me. Thought I'd just keep on getting everything
right, that I'd go to university and get some really good job,
meet Mr Right and get married . . .*

*Looks like a stupid dream you have when you're a kid,
now. Like being a ballerina or a spy. I'm close to four
months' pregnant and I don't even know who the dad is.*

*I saw Sophie at school today, and I hated her more than I
ever knew I could hate anyone. She was the only one I
trusted, I thought she was my best friend. And she didn't
even listen, never mind care. Hasn't spoiled her plans any.
While I've been throwing it all away, she's been doing all the
right things with that little group of clean-cut buddies I
always see her with – heading for a nice, smooth, easy future
and not a care in the world.*

God, I hate her.

*Anyway, what I've been meaning to say is, I've decided to
kill myself. Don't know what else to do, and it's not like
there's much to live for. Can't face telling Mum I'm
pregnant. Can't face going to school in maternity clothes.
Can't face life any more.*

*I know Mum's got sleeping pills. And I can easily get
served with the whisky.*

I'll do it tomorrow. In the night.

1

Friday, August the twenty-second. The pub was busy at lunchtime. Inside, it was too hot, too oppressive. The wooden benches outside were packed almost solid.

'So how's it going?' asked Kate, sitting at one across from Sophie and setting her drink down. 'Haven't had a chance to talk to you properly in *ages*.'

'Oh, not so bad.' Sophie smiled. 'I'm working hard, of course, but it's good fun.'

'Shame we don't get to see more of each other. You don't have much to do with the account handlers, do you?'

'Not really.' Sophie didn't want to say what she did next, but somehow had to – the world had become ominously quiet on the subject. 'Haven't even seen Rachel in weeks – do you know what she's up to?'

'Jesus. Haven't you heard?'

Sophie stared. 'Heard what?'

'She's gone. Got fired three weeks ago, nearly.'

'You're joking.'

'No shit. I don't know exactly what happened. Apparently she'd been screwing up for a while, then didn't show up for this big pitch she was supposed to be leading.' Kate's eyes were round, nakedly curious. 'I can't believe you didn't know. She's your cousin.'

'We've never been close.' It was a knee-jerk response that came out on its own. Sophie was suddenly and profoundly uncomfortable. 'So what's she doing now?'

'Christ knows. I called her at home a few times, after I heard, but I just got her answerphone. Left messages for her to call me back, but she never did. Maybe she's too busy looking for a new job.' Kate broke off for a second, took a long, deep breath. 'It's so weird, you know, I always thought Rachel was like Superwoman.'

'Yeah,' said Sophie slowly. 'I did too.'

'Oh well. Expect she'll bounce back. She's got Andrew to see her through it, after all – he seems like a nice guy.'

'Yeah.' Sophie felt herself flushing, and raced clumsily to change the subject. 'You having anything to eat here?'

'Might as well. Get fed up with that free Pret stuff every day.'

'You're lucky,' said Sophie. 'The sandwich guy never comes round to the admin bit,' and Kate said, well, she might work her way up, and they laughed, and the conversation moved on cheerily, leaving Rachel behind.

But back in the office that afternoon, Sophie found that her creeping fears wouldn't go away; formless as shadows, fed and nurtured by guilt. She had an overwhelming sense that Rachel knew all about it – she remembered the look Rachel had given her in reception, when she'd come out of the lift and seen her talking to Kate. The naked, chilling hatred in those eyes. It was as if she'd seen Rachel's mind working, moving back to a patch of shadow behind a garden shed – her own instinctive and horrified recoil from Rachel's words...

But she was being silly. Nearly a month had gone by since that encounter. If Rachel was going to try and get back at her somehow, she told herself, she'd have done something by now. It was the same rational inner voice that tried to explain odd noises in the dead of night; it deliberately refused to define *something*.

At half six, she left the building and headed towards Farringdon station. Andrew was cooking for her that night, as he had done last Friday, and the Friday before – already, their relationship had begun to set into routine. It soothed and disturbed her simultaneously. As her affection for him deepened, the weight of private knowledge had become heavier and heavier. Things she'd never told anyone, had never even *dreamed* of telling anyone – things that would almost certainly drive him away.

Rachel's hating eyes. The reasons for that hatred. The events that had ultimately changed both of them. The longing to confide at last, unburden herself of secrecy. Maybe she'd be deserted, but at least she'd be *understood* – for as long as Andrew didn't know those things, he didn't really know her at all.

I'll tell him tonight, she thought starkly, then, *but how can I? It's impossible. Where could I start?*

At the beginning, of course. It was the only place there ever was.

Sophie changed lines at King's Cross and got the tube to Fulham, feeling resolution weaken, strengthen, weaken again as the minutes passed. It seemed no time at all till she was there. She walked through a network of quiet, leafy residential streets till Andrew's flat came into sight, and she crossed the road towards it.

2

She was crossing the road. The golden light of early evening was tinged with sepia shadows, combining with the tree-lined street to create the perfect picture. Innocent, carefree prettiness, blonde ponytail swinging as she walked.

Rachel sat behind the wheel, unmoving, eyes fixed on the girl in the distance. She was parked at the side of the road, maybe a hundred metres from Andrew's front door. The MG was anonymous here, just one of many shiny new cars. She'd only have it for another month, till her court appearance in September. It didn't matter. By then, she'd have done all she needed to.

She watched Sophie approach the front door and ring the bell. In her mind's eye, she could see the staircase she'd seen so many times before; the dark-green carpet, the cream-coloured walls, Andrew hurrying down in jeans and a sweater. Then her attention switched back to the girl on the doorstep, the door opening, the tiny hint of Andrew that said it all. She saw mouths moving round words she could imagine too clearly before Andrew stepped back, and Sophie stepped in, and the front door swung shut.

It was always the same now, on Fridays. She'd come here every Friday for the last month; before she'd lost her job, she'd left work early just so she could be here, keeping watch from a distance. A part of her had known that Sophie would arrive when *she'd* used to, and she had. Andrew would be cooking dinner tonight, just as he'd used to cook for *her*. She remembered his stock dish, the one he was best at and repeated endlessly – spaghetti bolognese. She wondered if it was waiting in the kitchen right now.

The tears should have come then. But they didn't. Hatred had become her only emotion; she woke with it at eleven or twelve each morning in the bedroom that didn't look quite so perfect any more, lay for hours in the tangled sheets and felt it burning inside her. She drank with it till the small hours every night. It told her that the loss of her job didn't matter any more than the imminent loss of her licence, than the money that wasn't coming in any more. It told her there was only one thing that still mattered in the world.

When she found messages from Nina on her answerphone and forced herself to call Nina back, the hatred kept the words coming, the easy references to Andrew and the office. It enabled her to maintain a façade down the phone, knowing that it was no longer important. She could have maintained that façade in the middle of a total breakdown, for as long as Nina couldn't see her. When Nina said she sounded a bit distracted, she blamed it on the pressures of work.

The hatred was in her veins and it throbbed along with her heartbeat: *Sophie, Sophie, Sophie.* And she sat in the silence of her car as the evening came down, and felt its presence beside her. She was certain, now. It had guided her. The time for planning had come.

She sat until darkness descended and the light went on in Andrew's kitchen, and she saw the hint of their shapes in the window. Then she started the engine and drove home. She was efficient as an automaton now. Fear had stopped existing.

When she let herself into the flat, she went straight to the phone, and called Peter.

3

They'd just finished eating the spaghetti bolognese he'd cooked, and were sitting at the kitchen table drinking red wine. From the corner of his eye, Andrew found himself watching Sophie closely. She'd been strangely quiet all night, he thought, looking at him as if for a cue that hadn't come. Now she set her glass down, and spoke tensely.

'Andrew – there's something I've got to tell you.'

He'd known it was coming, even though he didn't have the slightest idea what it was. He tried to find some clue in her expression, but read only determination and thinly veiled fear. 'What's the matter?'

'It's something you asked me ages ago. What happened to Rachel. I don't want to talk behind her back, but there's no other way I can tell you.'

She'd never really taken him by surprise before, but now she did. They hadn't mentioned Rachel's name for weeks. 'What is it?' he asked her at last.

'It might make you think of me differently. You might decide you don't want to see me any more. I don't know *how* you'll react.' She spoke calmly; only her eyes betrayed her apprehension. 'But I've just got to tell you. I keep thinking about it.'

He looked at her, not knowing if he wanted to hear this or not, forcing himself to believe he did. 'Tell me.'

'It happened when I was ten years old. Rachel was eleven. Her mum's new boyfriend invited her mum on holiday for a month – just her mum, not Rachel. From what Rachel told me, I don't think her mum really wanted to go, at first.

'But Rachel told her she'd be fine, she could stay with me. I asked my mum if she could, my mum said sure. We were best friends at the time, and thought it would be great spending the whole summer together. Like being sisters.

'Only when she arrived, it wasn't a bit like I'd expected. She got kind of withdrawn after she'd been staying a few days. After the first week, she was hardly speaking to me. I couldn't understand it. She couldn't seem to stand the sight of me, but she had these times when she just *followed* me everywhere. You know, if I had to go upstairs and get something, if I'd left something out in the garden. If I went to the *loo*, she'd come up and talk to me through the door. It drove me mad.

'I never noticed at the time, but she was only like that when my dad was in the house. The rest of the time, she seemed much happier on her own. Never wanted to do anything together.

'Well, when she'd been staying a week and a bit, we got a call to say Great-Aunt Lily had died. She was my dad's aunt, not my mum's, but my mum treated all his family like they were hers. She was closer to them than *he* was, I think – always dragging me round to their houses for Christmas and Easter and God knows what. Auntie Jen. Uncle Tony. Gran and Grandad.

'Mum wouldn't have dreamed of missing the funeral, even though it was miles away. We had to stay with Gran and Grandad for a week or so after it, she said, they'd be so upset, they'd need the company. The funny thing was, Dad said he couldn't go. He was a police inspector, said he couldn't just take leave at the drop of a hat. At the time, it didn't occur to me, but I remembered later – he'd told me once about a man he worked with getting compassionate leave when his uncle

186

died. He was an inspector too.

'Mum couldn't get in touch with Rachel's mum. All we knew was that she was in Corfu; didn't even have an address for her, never mind a phone number. My mum was really worried, said what was she going to do, she couldn't possibly take Rachel to a family funeral. It wouldn't have been the normal thing to do, you see, the conventional thing. She was like that about everything, my mum.'

Sophie broke off. Andrew watched her take a deep breath, sip at her wine. Not a word was spoken for endless seconds.

'Dad said he'd take a standby week – something like that, anyway, I can't quite remember. It meant he could stay home, but had to be on call the whole time in case something happened. He said that way he could make sure Rachel was all right – it was like she was three years old, not thirteen.

'It seemed like a good idea. I couldn't understand why Rachel seemed so upset about it. It wouldn't be much fun for her, but she wasn't the kind of girl who wanted fun fun fun all the time. A few days before we were due to go, I said I'd send her a postcard if she liked, and she looked like she was about to burst into tears. She got really moody. Didn't speak to me for a whole day.

'I was kind of worried about her, but she wouldn't tell me what was wrong when I asked. After that, I just tried to forget about it. I'd never been close enough to Great-Aunt Lily to feel upset, and I was quite looking forward to going away. We'd be staying round Gran and Grandad's, and I liked it there.

'The day before we were due to go, I was out in the back garden, on the swing. She came out and said she had something to tell me. I was curious, and she said it was a secret. We went behind the shed, where it was private and the grown-ups couldn't hear us even if they came into the garden.

'She told me Dad had been – touching her, whenever they were alone together. She said she didn't want us to go away, for fear of what would happen. She said she was sure that was why he'd decided to stay, and she couldn't stand to be alone with him, and I could say I had the flu or something – I could stay after all, it would all be okay then.

'I just couldn't believe what she was saying. I felt sick. It was horrible, it made me want to throw up. I hated her for making me feel like that. I told her she was lying and ran away – went back into the house, locked myself in my room.

'We never spoke to each other again, not properly. Not till we met earlier this year.'

Silence. She took another sip of wine, swallowing it like medicine.

'But all the time we were at Gran and Grandad's house, I just couldn't get it out of my head. Kept going over and over it. Rachel wasn't a liar, she always told the truth. And then I remembered her following me around whenever Dad was home, and the way she'd stopped talking to me that first week. The grown-ups kept asking me what was wrong, but I couldn't tell them. How could I?

'And it got worse after we came home. I wasn't friends with Rachel any more, but I still saw her in school almost every day. She was like a different person. She started hanging round with a bad crowd, sleeping around – I heard rumours on the grapevine, you know how it is at school. It was nothing like Rachel, not the Rachel I'd known. She'd been head girl at our primary school, she always did the right things. And then I knew what I suppose I'd really known all along. It was true. When we'd been at Gran and Grandad's house, my father had raped her—'

She broke off, took a deep, shuddering breath. Andrew watched her across the table, appalled.

'Mum and me had been close before. But that all changed. Every time I looked at her, I knew she had no idea what had happened, and she started to feel like a stranger. It was the most important thing in the world to me, and there was no way I could tell her any of it. How can you tell your mum something like that? Especially a mum like mine. She was shocked if someone used a swear-word on telly. If a sex scene came on, she always changed the channel straight away.

'As for Dad, I could hardly even look at him. Every time he

touched me, my skin just crawled. I hated being alone with him. I knew how Rachel must have felt, that summer...

'But I was too scared to move out. Even when I was eighteen and I was supposed to. I was always scared of things after that. I'd used to think home was safe, and look what had happened *there.* I didn't want to go somewhere else, I might find other things like that, even worse things. I just wanted to stay where I'd been when I was a kid, when I'd been happy.

'Dad died in a car crash, two years ago. My mum cried at the funeral. I tried to, but I couldn't.' She broke off, took a deep breath. 'I kept thinking about Rachel. And I always felt so guilty, that it was my fault – if only I hadn't run away like that, if only I'd stayed, or told someone. When I came to London, I just wanted to make sure she was all right now—'

Her voice caught on the last word. Her head bowed and she started crying: hoarse, racking sobs that seemed forcibly dragged from her. He got up quickly, went over, put an arm round her shoulder.

'It's all right,' he said quietly. 'It wasn't your fault. Christ, Sophie, whatever you did wrong, it sounds like you've paid for it a hundred times over. It was a terrible thing for both of you, I'm not going to judge you, you were *twelve years old.*'

She cried a while longer. He knew this had been festering inside her a long time, and didn't try and make her stop. Just held, and comforted, and tried to understand. He had a momentary image of Rachel like something locked out in the cold, outside a well-lit window. Guilt stabbed him hard in the chest, out of nowhere. *What if she'd told me her side of the story?* he wondered. *What if I'd understood her better, what if I'd known?*

But he knew there was no point wondering. It was far too late to go back. This was his life now, and he'd made his decision – the flat in Fulham, the lamplight in the kitchen, the woman at the table, her shoulder fragile and shuddering beneath his hand. He cast Rachel out of his mind for good, forcing guilt away like an intruder. For better or worse, he had chosen.

4

Six thirty on Thursday evening. The Turk's Head was getting busier. They were sitting at a back table in the corner, talking in low, hushed voices. She supposed the casual observer would have taken them for lovers.

'I'm sure of it,' she was saying. 'She'll be there tomorrow evening, between seven and half past. It's a quiet street. There's hardly ever anyone around.'

He watched her intently. She kept expecting questions, but none came – kept discovering them in her own mind, answering them herself. 'There's a little park across the road from the front door. You can wait and watch from there.'

Unexpectedly, he spoke. 'I'll need a photograph.'

'I don't have a photograph. She looks about seventeen or eighteen. Dark-blonde hair, usually tied back in a ponytail. About five foot three. Size eight.'

'I'll recognise her,' he said.

She looked at him, trying to analyse his mood. There was something different about him tonight, something that was hard to place. The fleeting animation she'd seen from time to time in his eyes had become a constant presence, almost a sparkle. If she hadn't known him or the situation, she'd have thought it made his face more pleasant, more human, engaging. Even in the depths of her new indifference, she found that look disturbing.

'Good,' she said. She lowered her voice even further, speaking in a half-recognised attempt to reassure. 'Nobody's ever going to be able to trace it back to you, so long as you're not seen – even if you *are* seen, and you run. There's no link between you. You don't even know her name.'

He was smiling now. 'I'm not scared.'

She looked at him closely. 'I'll be back in a minute,' she said. Down the gleaming wood stairs, she headed into the Ladies'.

A couple of girls were gossiping at the mirrors, and she heard their muffled voices through the cubicle door. 'So I was just *shocked*,' one was saying. 'I couldn't *believe* she nicked it from Boots.' As Rachel came out, she had a glimpse of them before the doors swung shut, leaving her alone in silence.

She washed her hands, seeing her reflection under the harsh white lights. She was looking terrible, she saw – it was as if hatred had sucked the colours out of her, leaving her pallid and fragile. It occurred to her all over again that Peter hadn't seemed to notice. He hadn't even asked her about her dismissal; when she'd told him she'd left, he'd asked no questions. He didn't really see her, she thought, took no genuine interest in her at all. It was as if he looked for his own reflection in her only.

More than ever, she felt his unfathomable sickness – had the sense that she was making a pact with some enigmatic urban devil. She realised she didn't care. All that mattered was that Sophie's death would take place tomorrow night, that this crippling hatred would leave her, and she'd be at peace inside.

She stood for long minutes, and saw hatred look back at her. The only sound was a tiny, unplaceable buzzing that might or might not have been her imagination.

And constantly, constantly, the name pounding along with her heartbeat. *Sophie. Sophie. Sophie.*

5

When Peter let himself in that night, the communal room's door was ajar. He could hear the women talking beyond it, their laughter behind the canned-laughter track from a sitcom. It barely registered in his mind. He went up the stairs and shut himself into his bedsit, sat down on the bed and thought.

He had no desire to go for a walk tonight. The address Rachel had given him was tucked in his jeans pocket, the directions she'd given him recorded in his head. Tomorrow evening, it would happen for real. The anticipation he felt was more intense than anything he'd known or even suspected – his life trembled on the brink of epiphany.

She looks about seventeen or eighteen, he remembered. *Dark-blonde hair, usually tied back in a ponytail.*

It never occurred to him to wonder who she was. It could have been his own sister, for all it mattered to him; an account director at BHN, a counter-hand in Pret. They'd all become the same in his eyes, except Rachel. She wasn't at BHN any more, but that wasn't important; he had no interest in what had caused her to leave, so long as he still saw her. She was a part of him, and he adored her for that reason alone; she proved his potential to love.

The world would never understand his feelings for her, their depth, their reality. If other people knew, they'd bring his love down to the only level they understood – and they'd be wrong, completely wrong. He'd never had the slightest wish to sleep with her. That was an integral part of all he hated; he only needed to hear the way other people talked about it, the way it was described in the films and songs and magazines they liked. The boys at school, sniggering over a dirty joke. Shagging, fucking. Loathed.

He'd always felt the same way, even in the classroom. Before he'd known what love meant. An absolute and instinctive revulsion towards the words and what they implied – sweaty, cider-fuelled tangles against walls and bushes in the night, the essence of all he despised. The idea of it twining around him, embodied by Claire or Jeanette or Tiffany. He'd sensed humanity and mindlessness in those girls like a contagious disease, a simultaneous invasion and corruption of self.

But the gun ... that was different. As they'd moved into puberty, the other boys had had Page Three and battered old *Playboy* centrefolds. Only he'd had something more ...

Grandad ashen and crumpled in a hospital bed, the curtains pulled round it, obscuring. The hoarse, rasping whisper of his voice. *You're the only one I'd trust to have it, Pete boy. You know where it is. You'll know to be careful with it, won't you?*

He'd always known it was the key to something immense. And now, at last, he had found the door.

Tomorrow, he thought, *six thirty, Fulham.* From the room next door, he could hear the closing credits of *The Weakest Link.* He sat on the narrow single bed, poised and unmoving, like something rabid preparing to taste blood.

6

This time tomorrow...

Rachel sat at the kitchen table, pouring vodka over tonic and ice. Everything around her had become clearer, more vivid – the colours brighter, reality somehow heightened. She sat and drank and felt the future appearing as she watched – dead Sophie, Sophie dead, the hatred and the past finally over...

And the gradual approach of new hope, unexpected and glorious. The idea that with Sophie gone, it might be possible to go back, rebuild, return to what she had been. There was, after all, a precedent: eleven years ago it had looked as hopeless as this, and it hadn't destroyed her.

The bright, hard light of the little bathroom back in Underlyme. One o'clock in the morning. Getting Nina's sleeping-pills out of the bathroom cabinet, the bottle of whisky set down on the floor. Thinking about writing a note, but not quite knowing what to say; her old diary would have said it all, but she'd thrown it out yesterday. Her mind a chaos of conflicting emotions, images of the Townsends flashing like a strobe light behind her eyes.

Unscrewing the cap on the sleeping-pills, swallowing, swallowing. Whisky helping them down, burning her throat. Initial nausea fading as she forced herself to drink again and again. A sleepy feeling, the world and strong emotion drifting away as she watched. A distant amazement at the painlessness of it all. If this was dying, dying didn't hurt in the least . . .

Ironic, really, the factors that had saved her. The tiny flat had toilet and bathroom in a single room, and the bolt on the door had been broken. Nina woke in the middle of the night and went to the toilet, found Rachel unconscious, called an ambulance. Nina told her that later, when she knew about the pregnancy. The doctors had told Nina about the baby before Rachel could regain consciousness and plead with them not to.

Not that there was a baby any more. Rachel had nearly died herself. The doctors told her it had been touch and go for three days.

How she felt, when they told her. An overwhelming and dizzying sense of reprieve – the greatest wonderment she'd ever known in her life. She was alive and she wasn't pregnant and she had the chance to do it all again. It wasn't too late to begin a different kind of life. When she got back to school, whispers behind her back told her news of the pregnancy had seeped out somehow. It didn't concern her. All she wanted was to get out, start again somewhere else.

Breaking off with the bad-news gang, rediscovering the library just in time for GCSEs, getting just the grades she needed to go on to sixth-form college, then two As and a B at A level. The delight of the acceptance letter from Exeter University. The years of study culminating in the 2:1, the graduate training scheme at Markson Vickery. Brief relationships heavily shadowed by a dark bedroom and a long hot summer, before Andrew Megson arrived and she realised even *that* part of her life hadn't been damaged beyond repair. Even though she'd never feel entirely comfortable with sex and always needed the light on, she was *capable* of sex. She could fall in love with a man. She'd broken free . . .

It had happened once. Why not again? When Sophie wasn't there any more, the world would look different. She might even get over Andrew's loss. In time . . .

This time tomorrow, Sophie's going to be dead.

Rachel sat up, and drank, and remembered, and prayed. She felt tomorrow coming closer.

7

At half past ten on Friday morning, the phone went on Sophie's desk. She knew it would be Andrew, and it was.

'Hi, Sophie. How's it going?'

'Oh, not so bad. Busy,' she said. 'How are you?'

'Much the same. You still on for tonight?'

It had taken on the feel of a pleasant ritual – he always asked, she always was. 'Of course.'

'Well, I'll see you about seven-ish then. Have a nice day.'

'You too,' she said. 'See you then.'

Sophie hung up, and realised she was smiling. The extent of her happiness hit her out of nowhere. She couldn't believe it had only been a week since she'd told Andrew everything. Ever since then, she'd had an extraordinary sense of freedom – no matter how mundane their daily conversations were, they never failed to remind her that she'd done the right thing. She'd never known that she could feel this much a part of someone else, that she could trust a man this completely; a depth of affection she'd forgotten existed, a happiness she hadn't really felt since childhood.

She'd never understood the full weight of her guilt before. Over the years, it had grown to feel as much a part of her life as breathing. Only now it had been lifted from her did she realise how it had been pulling her down. A constant shadow over small pleasures, too familiar to recognise – her own voice coming back to accuse her in a dream. *You're lying!* she shrieked, and with the words came a crawling and helpless culpability; something shameful beyond expression, demanding the rest of her life in penance . . .

No longer. It was as if, by sharing the truth with Andrew, she'd finally seen it through impartial eyes. *You were twelve years old,* he'd said. *Whatever you did wrong, it sounds like you've paid for it a hundred times over.* And it amazed her all over again to realise the truth of those words. She *had* been a child at the time, it *had* haunted her life ever since; at last, she honestly believed that she deserved to forget.

And with her guilt went her fear of Rachel, of an unknown vengeance lurking in the shadows. Rachel would have moved on by now, she thought – found a new job, even a new man. The unease she'd felt about Rachel's disappearance had been no more than paranoia; that part of their lives was over.

Checking her watch, she saw it was ten past twelve. She realised she was hungry. Her journey towards the lifts took her through the main account-handling section of the office, and she saw that the seldom-seen young man was making his lunchtime rounds – Jessie's brother, she remembered, the troubled loner. In the clarity of her joy, she was alert to people, and looked at him closely. He didn't look like the kind of person Jessie had implied at all, she thought; he looked every bit as happy as she felt inside.

He was gone from her thoughts almost immediately. She walked on, towards reception and the bright afternoon, looking forward to that evening, Fulham station, another easy, magical Friday-night dinner with Andrew.

8

Peter left work early, claiming a doctor's appointment. It was half four when he let himself into the house. Heat and sunlight had intensified to become a presence in their own right, something drowsy, sensual, replete. He headed through the hallway quickly, cold inside with excitement.

They put you in prison for things like that, Pete boy, Grandad said in his ear.

In his bedsit, he knelt on the carpet, extracted the bottom drawer; took out the holster, then the pistol. On a cerebral level, he'd always understood its potential, but for the first time he understood everything it meant. He rose to his feet, and stood looking at death in his hand.

He put the safety catch on. He put the pistol in his pocket and pulled the concealing sweater over his head. He replaced the bottom drawer, went back downstairs and left the house.

On the tube to Fulham, he stood on platforms and waited, seeing the garish posters around him with new eyes. How easily they could be destroyed, they and all they represented. *Bacardi Breezer. Wonderbra. Revlon.* He carried an end to it all in his pocket, and the knowledge brought a sense of imminent metamorphosis – he had no idea what he was to become, only that the change was inevitable, and he longed for it. Rattling trains and the world hammering in his ears. For the first time, he felt it all, tasted it all. He was alive.

Out of Fulham station, he followed the directions Rachel had given him until the street signs became familiar. Carlisle Road, he remembered, and crossed the road towards it. The narrow, tree-lined street was deserted. He headed towards the little park he could see ahead, looking at the houses on the other side of the road. Number 21, Rachel had said, and he saw it at last – a green-painted front door with a shiny brass knocker, a discreet little burglar alarm, closed iron gates waist-high. It didn't stand out from the houses around it at all, but to him, it had become the only one that existed.

He turned and walked through the open gates, into the little rectangle of park. It had an overcrowded look, and at this time of day was heavily shadowed by neighbouring houses. The grass was dark and damp-looking, and clumps of pallid rhododendrons pressed in on a narrow strip of path. The bench was just inside the gates, facing through the railings, on to the road. Peter sat down on it. A pigeon strutted across the path by his feet. Otherwise, the stillness was undisturbed.

He checked his watch. Quarter to seven.

He sat, watched and waited. Brief flickers of movement caught his attention, discarded it again instantly. A middle-aged woman walking a black poodle, turning the corner and vanishing from sight. An empty street for five minutes. A noisy group of teenagers hurrying along, their voices lingering a long time in the distance. An empty street for three minutes. A black Audi sports turning into the road, pulling up at the kerb – a youngish man getting out, letting himself into one of the houses. An empty street for eight minutes, before another flicker on the outskirts of his vision made him turn his head.

A young woman approaching, on the far pavement. Eighteen at most, he judged – maybe five foot three, size eight. She had dark-blonde hair. It was tied back in a ponytail.

Inevitable, that she would stop at number 21. But still, he had to wait until she did so. He watched her approach it, observing as if in slow motion. Every step she took, every bounce of her ponytail seemed to last a minute. Part of him was aware that he was standing up, taking the pistol from his pocket, flicking off the safety catch even as he watched, enthralled.

She was opening the waist-high gates now, letting herself in. Stepping up to the green front door with the shiny brass knocker.

Peter took aim and fired.

Across the road, the blonde girl crashed to the ground, blood pumping across the bland white stone of the doorstep.

9

Rachel woke up abruptly, as if she'd had cold water thrown over her. She sat bolt upright in bed. She hadn't drawn the blinds last night, and the room was flooded with the sunshine of a beautiful Saturday morning, approaching the end of summer. The clock by the bed said it was almost eleven o'clock.

Jesus Christ. I started drinking yesterday afternoon – I must have passed out before I could call—

The greatest apprehension she'd ever known in her life –

giddy, nauseating, almost unbearable hope. She barefooted her way to the hallway phone, pressed out Peter's number with fingers that didn't feel like hers.

The ringing tone echoed in her ear for endless minutes before a voice came on the line – a male voice, a stranger's voice. 'Yeah?'

'Can I – can I speak to Peter Mott, please?'

'Just a minute.' A moment's silence, the voice calling somewhere in the distance. 'Peter. Phone for you.'

A door closing, footsteps approaching. They disorientated her as if she heard them blindfolded. At last the phone was picked up again.

'Hello?' she said hesitantly. 'Peter?'

'I've done it.'

Freedom broke over her like a wave. When she spoke again, her voice trembled. 'Are you sure?'

'It's in the paper. Look in the *South London Press*, if you don't believe me – I saw it this morning. Her picture's on the front page, the girl I killed.' He laughed. 'Expect shooting's too common in London to make the nationals.'

She'd never heard him sound like this before; good-humoured, utterly reckless. 'For Christ's sake,' she said urgently, 'keep your voice down. You're not alone in the house, are you?'

'It's okay. There's nobody else around, they're all in their rooms.' He spoke casually, offhandedly. 'They don't matter. They don't know I killed her.'

He was standing in a hallway somewhere speaking those words, where people could step out and hear at any second. She felt the reality of his existence at this precise moment, and it terrified her. 'Don't talk about it. Whatever you do, don't talk about it while they're there. It's dangerous.'

'Do you think I care about that?'

A moment's silence, leaden with foreboding. 'You should do.'

'I don't. Not any more.' A happy, relaxed voice. 'I've never felt like this, Rachel. Never in my life.'

The idea of hanging up had become virtually irresistible, as if replacing a receiver could sever the connection between them. She dreaded another casual reference to death. 'I'll go and buy the paper,' she said. 'I'll call you when I get back.'

After she'd hung up, she stood for some time, breathing slowly and deeply, trying to collect her thoughts. Then something came to her, with new and swooning relief: there was nothing in the world to link her with Peter. If his wildness continued, she could deny all knowledge of the crime. It would be his word against hers that he hadn't been aware of Sophie through work, that he hadn't been acting on his own initiative.

He didn't have her number. He didn't have her address. She never had to contact him again—

And Sophie was dead.

The thoughts changed everything in an instant. She was in the grip of wonderment all over again. She went into the bathroom and showered, headed into the bedroom, where she dressed with a little more care than she'd been doing recently. She should tidy up soon, she thought; she'd been letting the flat get a little out of hand recently. But there'd be time enough for that later. There'd be time enough for everything later.

She looked in the mirror, and saw her old self.

Behind the wheel of the black MG, she drove to Fulham; saw Saturday crowds outside pubs and cafés, revelling in the last days of August. How appalled they'd be if they knew what she'd done. But she couldn't regret a thing. She just needed to see that front page with her own eyes, to let the truth of what had happened fully sink in. Bypassing Carlisle Road, she made for a newsagent she'd visited sometimes in the old days, when she'd stayed with Andrew in the family flat.

Inside, it was cluttered and shadowy. A young Indian woman sat reading a magazine behind the counter, and didn't look up as Rachel came in. Rachel headed over to the newspapers stacked under the magazine racks. She scanned the piles for the *South London News*, then saw the front page and stood stock-still.

The headline screamed: GIRL SHOT DEAD ON DOOR-STEP.

The photograph showed Helen Megson.

10

'I just can't believe it,' Andrew said, as Sophie came back into the living room with a cup of tea. 'I keep thinking I'm going to wake up.'

Almost one o'clock. An oddly chaotic air hung over everything; the curtains were half drawn, the light was shadowy and strange. She put the cup down on the table in front of him, sat down herself.

'Was that your mum you were on the phone to just now?'

'Yeah. She and Dad just got into Heathrow, they're on their way. Of all the times they could have been on holiday . . .' He took a deep breath, let it out sharply. 'Expect they'll have to talk to the police as well. I don't know what they want to hear, those people. A violent ex, maybe. Something like that.'

Sophie had no idea what to say. She watched him looking absently across the room. The half-light was oppressive, funereal.

'Helen didn't have anything *like* that,' he said at last. 'She wasn't even supposed to *be* here, you know, she was supposed to be travelling for the rest of the year – just didn't like it, came back out of the blue. When I got in from work yesterday, I didn't expect to find her things here, or that note in the kitchen.'

Sophie knew. He'd told her all this yesterday night, but in the blankness of shock, he seemed to have forgotten. She could understand how he felt only too well. A dreamlike sense of unreality had descended as soon as she'd seen the ambulance flashing blue lights outside Andrew's door; as she'd come closer and seen a white-faced Andrew talking to a couple of policemen in the open doorway. A sense that things like this just didn't happen.

'She just went to a friend's house,' he said. 'Said in her note she was bored, she'd be back in the evening . . .'

His shell-shock was palpable. She went over to the sofa, taking his hand. 'Do you want me to go?' she asked quietly. 'When your parents get here?'

'Christ, no, Sophie. You stay,' he said. 'I just wish you could have met Mum and Dad under better circumstances—'

He was on the brink of tears, and she could sense him fighting to hold them back. She tightened her grip on his hand, but that seemed inadequate, so she hugged him awkwardly instead. There was gratitude in his submission to the gesture, but still he struggled not to cry.

'It's so crazy, all that stuff the police asked me. Like who her enemies were. She never had an enemy in the world, I'm sure of it.' His voice trembled slightly, and he broke off for a second as if to steady it. 'She was the sweetest kid you could hope to meet. Rachel didn't usually get close to people, but even she really liked Helen. Everyone liked Helen—'

Her arms tightened round his shoulders. He lowered his face, and she saw a tear running down his cheek. She comforted. She understood. She was there.

11

It had changed him more than he'd ever have believed possible. The act of pulling the trigger. It was as if he'd seen in black and white all his life, and suddenly saw in colour. It was as if he'd been deaf all his life, and suddenly heard the sounds life made.

Yet towards the act itself, he felt nothing but indifference. So simple it had been, so quick and effortless. It had taken on the shades of an infinitely symbolic act that had no practical significance. At a cerebral level, he was aware of the horror with which others would perceive it, but that awareness couldn't sink in beyond a certain point. He concealed his crime as casually as a small deception, a stolen pen. He named it in his mind as easily as he breathed – the house, the street, the murder.

And more than ever, he felt his distance from the world that would be appalled – people's reactions and beliefs and attitudes had become as bewildering as the customs of some arcane tribe. He heard voices around him, and they meant nothing. It was as if he had forgotten the language.

He kept thinking about going out again in the evening, bringing the pistol with him, making the old fantasy come true in Stockwell High Street. He'd thought it before, but had never understood it as he did now – there was nobody in the world who still mattered, nobody he couldn't kill as quickly and easily as the blonde girl in Fulham.

Except Rachel.

The phone rang in the evening, and he knew it would be her – but a stranger answered, and didn't call his name up the stairs. The phone rang the next evening, and he knew it would be Rachel, and the same thing happened. The phone rang the next evening, and the next, and the next, and the call from Rachel never came. The days trickled past like sand in a timer, turning into a week, and then a fortnight.

For the first time, he realised that he had no way of getting in touch with her. No phone number. No address. When he thought about her, he began to be troubled by a suspicion that – but no, he wouldn't think of it. For as long as he could evade it, he could persuade himself that she'd be in touch soon, and he could be happy.

But as the weeks stretched out, shadows lengthened and darkened in his mind. He travelled between BHN, Pret and Stockwell with a dawning sense of loss. And the new colours and sounds around him only heightened his isolation. His mirror image, his other self had fallen out of sight, leaving him alone in a world he no longer understood.

He began to forget Rachel's face. She began to look like the others.

12

It was the fourteenth of September, or perhaps the twenty-fourth. The days had all begun to blur together for him. His invisibility here made it irrelevant. None of the people at the desks looked at him closely enough to see how much he had changed, was changing.

One side of an earnest phone conversation from a distant desk, the steady rumble of the printer hard at work. The just-audible murmur of the air-con. 'I'll have the tuna salad,' one of the interchangeable people was saying, 'and the banana cake.' All he had to do was mark the pad and walk away, and that was easy enough. He had become a kind of automaton, the pistol a constant presence in his mind.

He walked on. The big, noisy redhead he saw every day was leaving her desk, putting on her jacket – there was a cold edge to the air outside; the slow, melting afternoons were over. She didn't glance at him as she headed out. He was about to walk past her desk when his glance across it took in an essential detail. An unstamped, addressed envelope by the keyboard, a name scrawled in big, untidy writing, unmissable as neon in a black-and-white world.

Rachel Carter.

Instantly, he was alert for watching eyes – a quick look to left and right told him he was unobserved. He picked the letter up and tucked it under his order pad before walking on. He finished his circuit of the desks, waited by the lifts, and went through reception without seeing a thing.

Outside, the streets were as they always were at this time, busy with queues outside sandwich shops, with little groups of office girls hurrying back to work. He sensed horror lurking on the outskirts of his life, and while he feared it, he also needed to be alone with it. He turned off from the main road, down a narrow side street that ended in a cul-de-sac. A faded sign promised TOP JOBS over a doorway alcove – the window next to it showed dark shadows, bare boards, an abandoned stepladder. He went into the doorway, tore the letter open and read.

Hi Rach, I thought I'd write because I'm getting a bit worried – I've tried to call you loads, keep getting your answerphone. Sophie told me the other day about her and Andrew, I'm so sorry, I didn't have a clue. Have you got a new job yet? I was thinking we ought to meet up soon, and—

Dawning horror as he took in the words. Realisation. Disillusionment. Betrayal. In a stranger's handwriting he saw his mirror image become something other – a part of the hated world, another face in the anonymous crowd. The people who talked about and thought about and wanted things he didn't understand. *Rach* and *Sophie* and *Andrew*; she had another life, beyond and apart from him. These people might mean more to her than he did, than he'd ever done.

The lack of a phone call hadn't driven the truth home. Her abbreviated name at the top of the lined blue paper did. She had used him and then walked away. The death of the unknown blonde girl was all she'd ever wanted, and his adoration meant nothing to her.

She had become worse than anonymous in his mind. In less than a minute, she had become personally hated.

Back towards the main road, he passed a street-bin, screwed up the letter and threw it in. He had no remaining interest in it. There was no point in returning to BHN. He headed for Farringdon station and waited on the platform. The envelope in his jacket told him Rachel's address, and all he needed to know.

When he got back to Tooting, he went up to his bedsit, took out the drawer, then the pistol. He put the safety catch on and the pistol in his pocket, pulled the concealing sweater over his head. He didn't replace the drawer. There was no need. He had no intention of coming back here. He was entirely alone now, and had only one purpose left.

Peter got the tube to Camden. From there, it was easy to hail a taxi. He unfolded the envelope and read out the address to the driver. He sat back, and waited for Rachel's flat to arrive.

13

The taxi stopped outside a modern apartment block, a four-storey affair of pale stone and plate-glass. The forecourt outside was overlooked by CCTV cameras, and was empty apart from a green Range Rover and a black MG. He expected most of the residents were at work.

He paid off the cab quickly. He could feel the world ebbing away from him even as its colours and sounds and textures intensified to become almost hallucinogenic; an overwhelming finality, a sense of apocalypse he'd never even felt in Fulham. He walked over to the intricate bank of doorbells and intercoms. Consulted the envelope again. *Flat 2*, he read. He pressed the buzzer, and waited.

When her voice came through at last, it sounded slurred, sleepy. 'Who's there?'

'It's me. Peter.'

'What do you want?'

'To come in. Let me in.'

No answer, but a small electronic *bleep* – he leant on the door, and it opened. Inside, across a wide, cool, red-carpeted foyer, was the door marked *2*. He knocked. It swung open silently at the touch. He stepped in.

He moved slowly through the hallway, heard the door click shut behind him. There was a stale smell on the air, faint yet all-pervading; as if the windows hadn't been opened for some time, as if the flat hadn't been cleaned in weeks. Passing an open doorway, he had a brief glimpse of kitchen, a table crowded with empty bottles, washing-up piled high in a sink. On the floor, by the wall, eight or nine flies buzzed round what looked like a discarded Marmite jar.

He became aware that he was walking on something, and looked down. A collection of postcards had been torn up and scattered over the hallway carpet. He saw torn triangles of handwriting, torn squares of blue sky and golden sand. He realised all the overhead lights were on, implying drawn blinds, drawn curtains.

The door at the end of the hallway stood slightly ajar. He pushed it open and saw her slumped in an armchair. She had aged twenty years. The empty glass by her hand made him suddenly aware of others, randomly dotted round the room. She seemed hardly sentient, but her eyes turned to watch him as he stepped towards her, apparently unsurprised, unconcerned by his presence here. He caught the raw and pungent reek of spirits.

'You killed her,' she said.

His mind reeled before the ultimate betrayal of this squalor. 'I *loved* you.'

'I killed her,' she said.

He drew the gun from his pocket. He flicked the safety catch off. He looked at her and saw indifference look back.

'I trusted you,' he said, and then he fired.

Epilogue

TEENAGE KILLER SUICIDE SHOCK

The teenage killer of 26-year-old advertising executive Rachel Carter was yesterday found dead in police custody. Peter Mott, 19, is believed to have hanged himself with his own belt.

Although Mott had been due to face a charge of manslaughter in two months' time, his motives have remained mysterious. Prior to his death, he had refused to comment on Miss Carter's murder, or explain his possession of the unlicensed pistol with which it was committed.

Mott was arrested eight months ago when Miss Carter's neighbour became alarmed, and summoned police to her exclusive Camden apartment block. 'I was off work with flu when I heard a gunshot,' said James Cheshire, 36. 'I called 999 right away.'

When police arrived at the scene, they discovered Miss Carter dead from gunshot wounds in her £200,000 flat, and Mott still present. 'It's hard to understand, even looking back,' said arresting officer Michael Collingwood. 'He could have run, but just stayed there. He didn't fight when we handcuffed him, and he'd thrown the gun down before we arrived. He didn't say a word.'

Although capable of speech and clinically sane, Mott never spoke again. For months, detectives have expressed their frustration at his silence. 'We're convinced he was also responsible for the murder of Helen Megson,' a Scotland Yard source told us yesterday, referring to the 18-year-old student shot dead on the doorstep of her Fulham home last August. 'But Mott refused to tell us anything at all.'

The parallels between the two deaths are certainly striking.

Miss Megson was killed only three weeks before Miss Carter, had no known enemies, and her injuries were unquestionably caused by the pistol in Mott's possession. Another link between the two cases would appear to rule out coincidence. Miss Carter was, shortly before her death, living with Miss Megson's brother.

In the light of Mott's ongoing silence, however, nothing has been proved. Now, with his death, it never will be . . .

THE TIMES, 4 DECEMBER 2003

The engagement is announced between Andrew, son of Mr and Mrs James Megson of Cobham, Oxfordshire, and Sophie, daughter of the late Mr Brian Townsend and Mrs Linda Ellis, of Underlyme, Dorset.

BRENT HARVEY NASH E-MAIL, 12 MAY 2005

TO: Team A; Team B; Team C; Team D
FROM: Diane Robinson
CC: Creative; Admin; Finance; Production
RE: Promotion

I'm very happy to announce Sophie Megson's promotion to Senior Account Manager. I'm sure you'll all join me in wishing her the very best.

18TH JUNE, 1988

I asked Sophie if I could come and stay in the summer holidays today, while we were sitting on the field in breaktime. She thinks it'll be great if I can, just like I told Mum. We're praying Auntie Linda says it's okay.

Don't think Uncle Brian's going to get involved, if she says no. Never really know what to make of him. I know it's stupid, but I never really like being on my own there when he's at home – when I come down from the toilet and have to go out through the back door and he's in the kitchen, when I have to get something I left in the lounge and he's alone in there reading the paper. Something about his eyes. The way he looks at me.

But that doesn't matter. I always love staying with Sophie, and it's only ever been evenings and weekends before. I'd rather be with her than anyone else I know. Everyone says we're just like sisters.

I'll know tomorrow. I'm meeting her by the gates, before school. She'll tell me then.